I AM KAVI

THUSHANTHI PONWEERA

HOLIDAY HOUSE · NEW YORK

TO RAJIV.
FOR ACCEPTING ME
AND WAITING PATIENTLY
WHILE I LEARN
TO ACCEPT MYSELF

STRINGS

A VILLAGE IN THE ANURADHAPURA DISTRICT,
SRI LANKA, MAY 1997

Jasmine

It's still dark outside when I wake up.
That time when there is not enough moonlight
or enough sunlight.

The jasmine flowers glow incandescent
as they always do,
eagerly looking for my outstretched hands.

I pluck them swiftly,
glad that their sweet-smelling scent
overpowers the smell of manure
drifting from the direction of the cows.

I carry them to the tiny altar
in the corner of our garden
and light a fresh stick of incense.

The serene face of
the small stone Buddha
reminds me
to practice loving-kindness.
I'd love to have that kind of face—
the kind that makes everyone feel
instantly calm.

Then I remind myself
that the Buddha took
years and years of
searching,
suffering,
enduring
to achieve
all that calm.

I am only ten.
Searching,
suffering,
and enduring
can wait.

Rituals

are like strings that connect
me to Amma.
At times,
the only ones.

I started drinking tea when I was a toddler,
Amma says,
begging for sips from her cup
till eventually I had my own.
I'm yet to be promoted
to the level of plain-tea drinker.
Mine consists mostly of milk
still warm from the insides of the cow

Amma milked
mere minutes ago.

We both drink our tea the same way.
One hand hugs the cup,
one hand stays open,
a bit of sugar in its palm.
A sip from the cup,
a lick from the palm.
Sip,
lick,
sip,
lick.

The comforting sounds of pirith
from the nearby temple surround us
as they do every day at dawn,
till the rooster crows,
breaking the reverie—
our signal to get moving.
Amma stands,
reties her hair into a bun,
tightens her redda—the cotton cloth
that hugs the lower part of her body—
and heads outside.

Kavi, wash up and come quickly.
She is referring to the empty cups.
Do it yourself.
I scowl back.
In my head of course.

Arguing with Amma is like
going to war.
You may win,
but not without a whole lot of
damage.

Daytime Amma

Daytime Amma
is not patient.

The grains fly out of her hands
as she throws them to the chickens,
gravy splatters her blouse while she cooks,
and the coconut-leaf broom swishes noisily
as she hurriedly sweeps the house.

I tell myself that
she may be faster
but that I do a better job.

I pause to pet the cows,
nuzzling their sweet noses,
thanking them for their milk;
and when I make mallung,
I cut the gotukola leaves as finely as possible
like you're supposed to.
When Amma makes mallung,
the pieces are so big
we might as well have

plucked the leaves off the ground
and eaten them straight.

Even our little front porch is spotless
after I'm done sweeping it.
I feel rather proud of myself,
though Amma keeps telling me to hurry up
and doesn't praise my work
like she used to.

Daytime Amma
is not patient.

The morning sunlight frames our shadows
as we walk past the cluster of small houses
around our own
and make our way to the common well.

This is where we wash—
ourselves,
our clothes—
to get ready for the day.
I, to go to school,
and she, to go to the paddy fields.

Amma draws the water,
the muscles in her arms pulsing
with each pull of the rope,
the metal bucket at the end of it
not spilling any water
thanks to her steady hands.

I tried doing it once,
but it was taking too long,
and by the time the bucket was up,
half its contents were out.

And daytime Amma
is not patient.

Siripala

At home,
my patience wears thin too,
as I try my best not to disturb
the sleeping lump of a man
covered in a sheet and
sprawled on the padura on the floor,
his tall body taking up
more space than it should.

I dress unhurriedly,
moving my arms slowly
through the sleeves of my school uniform,
the older one of the two I own,
hoping today won't be the day
it finally rips.

The sleeping lump yawns,
his eyes still closed.
I finish the rest of my dressing-up routine
in record time.

Hurry up, the food's getting cold,
Amma calls me.
Impatient again.
But this time
I'm thankful for it.

Anything to avoid
Siripala.

Incomplete

I step outside and walk around
to the back of the house,
dragging my hand over
its uneven wall and peeling paint,
to the makeshift kitchen
Thaththa built for us before he died.
It's incomplete,
missing half a roof
that Amma is saving up
to finish.

She hands me a plate of manioc,
our regular breakfast.
Mine is arranged into neat lumpy balls
pre-dabbed with grated coconut
to allow for the most efficient eating—
our special discovery.
I gobble them up,
finish tying my hair and shoelaces,
and bend down to worship Amma.

Another ritual.
Another string.

Sinhala-Buddhist

I used to fling myself at her feet,
my forehead to her toes,
arms clasped above my head,
knees and elbows on the ground,
no holding back.
Just like my religion taught me.
A good Buddhist girl.

I would do this
every day without fail,
unquestioning in my devotion to her,
my mother,
who could do no wrong.
Just like my culture taught me.
A good Sinhalese girl.

Not anymore

Lately,
there is no head-to-toe contact:
my knees hover inches away from the ground,
and I only graze her feet with my fingertips.
If she's noticed this lack of fervor
she hasn't commented on it.

Thunuruwan saranai,
she says as she touches my head,
calling the powers of the Triple Gem—
the Buddha, Dhamma, and Sangha—
to protect me.
I mutter the words back to her
not really meaning them.

Not so good anymore.

The lump is up

As I walk away,
I glance back to see her handing
a cup of tea to the man who is now awake,
his thin body leaning on the doorframe,
his sarong hitched up between his knees.

I walk faster.
My fists clench around
the strap of my school bag,
squeezing,
squeezing.

I really should try and step it up
with the loving-kindness.
They say it matters the most when
it's hardest to do.
And not to boast or anything,
but I've always been good
at the hard stuff.

Back then

It wasn't like this back then.
We were like those typical pictures of "My Family"
that kids are told to draw during art class.
Mother, Father, Child.
Amma, Thaththa, me.
Holding hands,
smiling,
always smiling.

Most of the fathers in the other kids' pictures
wore army camo
and carried a gun.
Mine did too for a few years,
until the uniform was replaced
with regular clothes,
and instead of two feet peeking out from
beneath the sarong,
I drew only one.
There was no gun hoisted on his arm
but there was a crutch.

It's what he came back with
after nearly a decade at the front lines.
The lower part of his leg had exploded
along with the Claymore mine he had stepped on.

Slow death

The news calls soldiers like him
"victims of the war,"
but the government awarded him a medal
and called him a hero.

He looked at it often,
twirling it in his hand,
while rubbing the stump below his knee,
his expression
changing over months from pride
to something I couldn't quite recognize.
Disgust?
Anger?
Regret?

But every night,
he held onto it while he slept,
that medal,
as if it were a part of him.
Something from the war to replace
something he lost.
Even the night he went to sleep
and never woke up.

Heart attack

So sudden!
So unexpected!
So young!

The people at the funeral seemed surprised
that Thaththa's heart had failed him.
The same people who had stopped
praising him,
visiting him,
inviting him.

Hadn't they failed him too?

Statues

I expected Amma
to be a bit more emotional
at the cremation
but she was pretty disappointing
to be honest.

She didn't wail,
fall on the ground,
tear her hair out,
or thump her chest,
like I've seen other widows do
when their husbands died in the war.

I crept closer to her,
hoping she would finally
break down and clutch me.
That we would sob together as one.
But she just stood there like a statue,
two steady rivulets of tears
pouring down the sides of her lovely face.

This meant that I couldn't cry either.
So, I swallowed my sobs
till my throat hurt.
I didn't want to give her
another reason to sigh
when she looked at me.
She'd been doing a lot of that lately,
and I knew she thought that I was
weak.

I wanted to show her
I could be a statue too.
Even if I was one
made of clay,
not fully dried,
and trying
not to
break.

The hidden pool of emotion

Amma is a statue made of rock.
Or so she likes to think.
But those tears must come from
somewhere.

Inside her is a hidden pool of emotion—
bubbling,
pure,
restless.

I remember
even though she seems to have
forgotten.

I remember
the deep throaty laughter,
the playful tickles,
and the hours spent being rocked on her legs,
her hands guiding my hands

as we
clapped
clapped
clapped

and she
sang
sang
sang.

After

It didn't even take six months.

Siripala was Thaththa's best friend.
Whenever my father stepped out,
he stepped in
to help with the cultivation,
the animals,
and to comfort my mother
whenever news of attacks came;
when we wouldn't know if Thaththa
had survived.

I guess Siripala
became Amma's best friend
just like he was Thaththa's.

After Thaththa died,
he stepped in
as usual.
But this time,
he didn't
step out.

But Thaththa isn't
replaceable,
like a tractor tire
or a faulty radio.
That's not how it works
with people.

Excuses

Amma tried explaining it to me.

Siripala doesn't have children.
He's a good man.
We need someone to look after us.
These times are unsafe.
Kavi, I can't do it alone.

I wanted to tell her,
You're not alone.
You have me.

But clearly
I wasn't enough.

Distance

She didn't try to explain after that.
Not even when I found a copy
of a fresh marriage certificate
making Siripala
officially my stepfather.

I cried,
screamed,
refused to talk to her,
ignored him.
Every day was a new opportunity

to make them as miserable
as I felt.

She would just close her eyes,
pinching the bridge of her nose,
till I finished
my rant.
Statue mode: activated.

Then she'd walk away.

As if Thaththa didn't mean
anything to her.
As if Siripala was the
love of her life.
As if she didn't care
how I felt.

She did this till the day
the village stopped gossiping,
I stopped ranting,
and everything went
back to normal.

Normal for everyone
but me.

Now

Sunset is my favorite time of the day.

Siripala doesn't come home from his job
at the army camp kitchen
till late at night.

Sunset will see Amma
seated on the floor of our porch,
her untied hair almost reaching the floor,
a comb tucked into it,
and the shape of her outstretched legs
visible under her redda, now loosened,
as she makes room for me between them
just like she did
when I was a baby.

This is when I get to have Amma
all
to
myself.

When the distance closes
for just a little while.

When my need to be near her
is stronger
than my anger with her.

The bare light bulb hanging overhead
makes everything golden
and the insects that hover around it
cast a dancing pattern on our bodies.
Our evening entertainment.

The exam

Amma's voice,
when it breaks the silence, is kind.
So, are you ready for the exam now?
I nod in reply,
too scared to say the wrong thing
that might ruin
this perfect moment.

The exam is the grade 5 scholarship examination.
The one that lets village kids like me
gain free entry
to a bigger and better school,
in a bigger and better city.

Not many of the parents in our village
agree to let their kids sit for it.
They prefer to have them around
to help with the fields and farming.
But Amma insisted I sit for it.
Education is the only way out,
she often says.
Out of what? I wonder.
She says I'll understand someday.

It's one of the hardest exams ever
and I've been studying all year.
I don't want to disappoint Amma,
and besides,
it's part of
my plan.

This exam is going to be
not just a way out for me
but for Amma too.

Nighttime Amma

is patient,
as if the darkness
has given her permission
to stop
and
breathe.

Her hands are warm and slick with coconut oil,
pungent with the smell of the fenugreek seeds
that soak in it.

Her palms
press and release
press and release
on my scalp
as she methodically
douses my hair with it

slowly,
steadily,
silently.

She retrieves the comb from her hair
and runs it softly through mine,
gently untangling any knots.
Finally, she gathers all of it,
now thick and heavy,
parts it into three,
and weaves the strands through her fingers,
plaiting it quickly and deftly.
I sigh.
It's coming to an end.

Stuck

The barbed wires that surround the army camp
are scraggly lines on the horizon
illuminated by the lights of the watchtower.
I can make out the silhouette of a soldier on watch,
the outline of his rifle clear,
jutting over his shoulder.

For a moment,
I envy his freedom to be
out there, making a difference,
while I'm stuck in here,
unable to change
anything.

Room

The air in the room is chilly at night,
and the sound of rain on our takarang roof
makes it hard for me to
fall asleep.
Tang,
tang,
tang,
the raindrops cry
as they fall onto the metal sheets,
and as the wind picks up,
water makes its way inside.
I wrap my sheet tighter around myself
and stand on the edge of my bed
so that I can reach the window
and pull it closed.

It's the only window on
my side of the room.

Our entire house is a room.
Or rather,
our room
is the entire house.

Except at night
when Amma's old sari is thrown
over the clothesline that goes across the middle,
forming a curtain—a line
dividing the house into my room

and their room.
Separating
my side
from theirs.

Sari and sarong

It's still cold.
I wish I could ask Amma
to close her window too.
But no way am I going to talk to her
when she's with him.
And tonight, she's with him.
Like really, really
with him.

I know this because, normally,
there is a gap at the end of the line
left by the not-quite-long-enough sari.

Tonight,
his sarong is draped there,
closing the gap to ensure
total privacy.

Sari and sarong.
Together.
Touching.

Yuck.

Not Done

I mean,
this is nothing new.
It's not rocket science.
I know what grown-ups do
behind the curtain.
Almost every house in our street
has a curtain.

At school,
we giggle about it.
And then we try and come up
with our own theories
of what actually goes on,
and the most likely one so far
is this:

Parents put up the curtain
when they want to kiss and hug
like the couples do in the Hindi movies
that we all watch with bated breath.
And like the movies,
we never really see anything because
just as the heroine falls into the hero's embrace,
blurry squares fill up the screen
till the scene ends.

Because children
cannot watch adults hug or kiss.
It is simply Not Done.

But we all know
that's what they do.

It's what my mother and father
did too.

But this is
not
my
father.

One year

It's Thaththa's one-year death anniversary,
which means we give alms to the monks
in his memory.
(Cook and serve lunch to them, basically.)
It's considered a
meritorious deed.
But all it is
is awkward.

I'm glad the temple is empty
so that there's no one to see
Amma's clear disrespect
to the memory of her dead husband
by letting her new husband
be a part of this.

I asked her about it this morning
while we drank our tea together.
Why does Siripala have to come?

Because he lost his friend too.
And because he's family!
Amma's response was unexpectedly emotional,
her voice getting louder
with each line.
She was choking back a sob.

A part of me enjoyed seeing her this upset.
Victory was close.
He may be family to you
but he'll never be family to me!

That's good
because I doubt he would have ever wished for
an ungrateful child
like you!
Her voice became hard
and her eyes turned cold
as my own filled with tears.

I should have known better.

No choice

The midday sun blazes down
as the three of us shuffle along in a row

serving food to the monks.
There are ten of them,
including a new one,
smaller than the rest,
barely older than me.
His orange robe keeps slipping off his shoulder
and he keeps shrugging it back into place.
I catch his eye and he smiles at me
even though he is not supposed to.

I don't mind.
I don't think he's supposed to be
living in a temple
with no friends,
no parents,
no freedom.
Not while he's so young.

I wonder if he didn't have a choice
in the matter.
Maybe we're both alike
that way.

Guilt

I sneak a look at Siripala.
He's bending down so much
that I worry he'll keel right over.
Trying to make amends probably.

I make sure to keep far enough away
from Amma and Siripala
so we don't look like a family,
but not far enough away
that I keep the monks waiting.
I am secretly thrilled
at this secret act of rebellion.
The *sili sili* noise of the bo leaves cheer me on.

I wonder what my father would think
if he could see us.
Would he think
I betrayed him too?

Unlike the visible layer of oil that remains
in the bowls of water that the monks wash their hands in,
my guilt is invisible
and I can't get rid of it
as easily as Amma has.

Once the meal is done and
the religious merits of the almsgiving
are offered to my father,
I excuse myself,
not waiting for Amma's permission.

I can't wait to get out of there.

PLANS
UNFOLDED

School

Weekend mornings
are usually spent at school
where extra lessons are held for those of us
sitting for the scholarship exam this year.

The path from the temple to school
is a straight line.
A straight line that goes
up a hill,
over a stream,
and through a jungle.

The sound of dry leaves crunching under my feet
and the soft gurgle of water
from the small stream alongside me
accompany me as I walk.
I push aside the yellow ehela flowers
that drip from the branches surrounding me,
not in the mood for their brightness.

The jungle only thins after what must be an hour
and my tangled mind clears
to match the landscape around me.

The vast stretch of land that my school sits on
is mostly bare,
with the exception of
random patches of grass
and a large, lone kohomba tree.

The building itself is just one floor—
a long set of classrooms
with half walls all around,
pillars to hold up the roof,
and wobbly screens in between,
allowing us to see the outdoors
from wherever we are indoors.
Paneless windows.

My spirits lift at the sight of it,
as does my waning energy.
I smooth my hair,
shake my slippers free of pebbles,
and walk in.

Curd and treacle

Good morning, Kavi!
You're the first to arrive!
Come, let me see your homework.

I love Nayana teacher.
She is sweet and kind and friendly,

but what she is most known for
is her complexion.

Nayana teacher is fair.
So fair her cheeks are almost pink;
so fair she's considered
the most beautiful woman in the village;
so fair that standing next to her
while she checks my work
makes me feel extra dark.
We're like curd and treacle—
milky white and golden brown.

Apparently, it's because she comes from Kandy,
a hill city in the middle of Sri Lanka.
According to Amma, that's where
all the beautiful people are born,
which can't be true
because Amma isn't fair
but she sure is beautiful.

Sunil

The other students trickle in.
The boys sit on one side of the class,
the girls on the other.

We have an inside game, us girls,
to ignore the boys as much as we can.

Just like they have a game
to annoy us as much as they can.

A paper ball missile
whistles out of its bamboo-stalk launcher
and lands between my fingers,
slick with spit.
I look up at Sunil
who grins back at me.
Then the boys tease him,
and the girls frown at me,
so it's eyes downcast again.

I like Sunil.
He prefers songs to silly jokes
and spitballs to pretend bullets.
And he's not afraid of showing it.
I wish I was more like him.

Nayana teacher raps the table twice
with her knuckles.
Let's begin, children!
she says in her musical voice,
and the room quietens
till the only sounds are the
staccato bleating of the goats
and the croaky cawing of the crows.
The slow and easy rhythm
of the village soundtrack.

Harmony

I love how everything works out
when I'm doing my lessons.

The words stick with me long after I read them,
complicated sums uncomplicate themselves,
and my answers are (almost) always correct.

If only I could solve Amma's problems
the same way.
But how can I?
The only problems she has
seem to be
with me.

Closer

I catch up with Sunil after the lesson,
I, walking faster than the girls,
and he, walking slower than the boys,
till we meet under the kohomba tree.

Reaching into the pocket of my dress
I pull out the paper ball, all dried up now,
and douse it with a generous dollop
of my own spit.

Here, Sunil,
I have to ask you something,

but I don't want the others to hear.
Come a bit closer, will you?

Sunil leans toward me
with questioning eyes.
That smile again,
so trusting.

You like them, don't you? I ask him,
trying hard to suppress the laughter
bubbling up my throat.

Huh? What do I like?
He stops and turns to me, confused.
A perfect target.
I pull the collar of his shirt
and drop the ball in,
clamping it in place with my palm
to really spread the spit around.

Spitballs! I shout
and take off,
Sunil hot at my heels.
We laugh all the way home.

Happiness not allowed

The laughter dies on my lips
when we reach my home
and I see him
again.

Siripala is squatting near the tap outside
washing the unwieldy pots and pans
that Amma used to cook food
for the almsgiving.
He must have taken the day off.

He pauses as we get closer,
shouts to make his voice heard
over the water-meets-metal din.
Ah, Sunil.
Did you hear that there was an attack
near your father's camp last night?

My head whips to Sunil.
Sunil with the smile that refuses to leave his face,
the smile that doesn't reach his eyes,
the smile that falters.
No. I hadn't heard.
But not hearing anything
is good, right?
He doesn't look so sure.
Siripala doesn't comment.
Just nods and goes back
to the pan at hand.

Siripala may not have a uniform or a gun
but he sure knows how to kill
happiness.

I have no idea what Amma sees in him.

Not all but some

I find Sunil by the stream
throwing rocks into the water.
Plip,
plip,
plop.

Did you find out?
I ask softly.

He nods.
He's okay.

For now,
he adds,
his mouth a hard line,
his eyes far away.
When I'm in the army
I'll be sure to get rid of
all those Tamils.
His voice is little more than a whisper
but his words seem so loud.

I grab some rocks and sit beside him.
Plip,
plip,
plop.

I don't like it when he talks like this.
It's so unlike him.
So harsh,
cold,
grown-up.

It's not all Tamils, no?
Just the LTTE.
Like our army.

Sunil scowls.
Are you saying that my thaththa
is the same as those evil people?
You don't mind that they're the reason
your thaththa was crippled?

No, that's not what I'm saying.
I think.
But I don't really know
what I'm saying
either.
So I don't say
anything.

Karma

Lord Buddha says that
hate will never cease with hate,
only with love.
But
all I see is hate piling on hate,
with no room left
for love.

Amma says that
those who harm us will get their due,
their karma.
But
don't we harm too?
Don't we kill too?
Won't our dues be
as bad as theirs?

If Sunil grows up
and goes on to hate and harm,
when will the war
ever end?

Revise, memorize

Nayana teacher keeps us back at school
longer and longer,
the closer we get to the exam.

We
revise,
memorize,
revise,
memorize

till the mosquito coil burns all the way through,
till the sun starts to set
and the flickering tube lights come on,
till the breeze blowing through the classroom
cools instead of warms,
till Nayana teacher swipes me on the head
with the pota of her sari
and calls out sternly,
If you want to sleep, Kavi,
go home!

But then she smiles
and shuts her books
and tells us we're done
for the day.

A seed

The morning that greets me
on the day of my exam
is sunny and promising.
It's going to be a good day.

Amma takes her time plaiting my hair,
exhaling noisily while she does,

so I know she's as
nervous
as I am.

She reaches into a tiny paper bag
and draws out two long, black ribbons.
She looks into my eyes and smiles
as she ties them to the ends of my two plaits.
Her smile is like water
to the tiny seed of hope
in my heart.

Hope is

what makes the weeks of
waiting for the results easier.
It makes the days fly faster
and the months seem shorter
and even makes Siripala
slightly more bearable.
Whenever my spirits fall,
hope is what gently lifts them up,
reminding me of how different
my future can be.
Hope is what makes me believe
that my plan
might actually work.

My plan

I'll get the best results,
just like I have
during every exam.
Amma will be so proud of me.
Then we'll both leave this place
and all its bad memories behind
and go to the city,
to my new school
where everything will be
fancy and new
just like in the movies.

Siripala won't be there.
Just Amma and me.
And nothing will ever
come between us
again.

Success

We got our results today!

I don't mean to boast or anything
but that good feeling I had about
how things would turn out?

Turns out I was right
because
I PASSED!

And not just by a small margin.
I have the best results of all the children
in our entire district!

Nayana teacher squeezes my shoulders
and tells me that this means
I am not just going to a better school
but that I can select which one.

I can't celebrate when I hear the news though
because Sunil has failed.
He takes one look at the list on the board
and walks away.

But as always
he's waiting for me
under the kohomba tree.

So, you'll go to the big city
and forget all about me, no?
He extends one gangly arm and
swats me on my head.
I guess this is his way of
congratulating me.

I worry that the city won't have a Sunil for me,
that there surely cannot be
a better friend than him anywhere,
but before I can answer,
he flings his foot through
a big mound of dust standing in our way.

Soon we are having a competition to see
who can kick up the biggest dust storm,
taking turns laughing and coughing.

If there were lessons on
How to Be Happy No Matter What,
I bet Sunil could teach them all
to me.

Finally

When Amma hears the news
she starts to laugh and cry at the same time,
neither of which she has done since, well,
I can't even remember.
She even draws me in for a hug
and my heart just about explodes with joy.
I hope she understands that this is my gift to her.
Our way out.

Choices

So which school shall I choose?
Would you like to live in Colombo,
near the sea,
or in Kandy, on top of the hills?

Where we live is
far from the sea
and nowhere near a hill.

Mostly it's just
flat,
dry,
boring.

This shouldn't be a
difficult choice for her.
Either option will be
fresh,
different,
exciting.

Baba

Amma sits down,
dabs at her face with a corner of her redda,
and starts wringing it
between her hands.
Not a good sign.

Baba, she says,
using the term of endearment
she saves for giving me
bad news.

*Baba, this rice will have to last us
the whole month.
Baba, Thaththa is injured.
Baba, Siripala is moving in.*

The parts of my exploding heart
crash down to earth.
I hold my breath.

I can't come with you.

My cheeks grow cold.
Why not?
She doesn't answer.
Amma, tell me.
Why can't you go with me?
I am angry.
Shivering,
shuddering,
wanting-to-shatter-everything
angry.

Just then, Siripala walks in.
With just one look from him,
her anxiety seems to dissipate.
I hate the way the shadows lift for him,
but not for me.

Ah, Kavi, I heard you did well.
Good for you, he says,
his smile breaking through all the lines on his face
making him look younger.

I look at Amma just in time to see her
give some sort of signal with her eyes
to Siripala, who promptly
leaves.

Déjà vu

This is supposed to be a celebration
but so far everyone is acting the same way
they did when they told me that
Thaththa was dead.

My heart starts beating faster.
I can tell something is wrong.
Amma's hand flits nervously to her throat
and then to her stomach.
Oh no, is she dying too?

Unexpected

Are you sick?
Suddenly,
it is suffocatingly hot.
Tell me!
I am ashamed at
the wanting,
the pleading,
the begging
in my voice.

Baba,
I'm pregnant.

The consolation prize

You can live with Mala Nanda.
She lives in a nice, comfortable house
and is happy to look after you.
Colombo is safer now, it seems, and
the house is close to the school.
You won't have to walk long distances alone
like you do here.
There is even a nice girl there
for you to play with.
Mala Nanda says there is
a big TV also.

Not consoled

It's not even Mala Nanda's house.
It's where she works.
As a housemaid.
And a big TV?
Really?
Does Amma think I can be
bought over that easily?

I'm running

so fast that
my heart pounds
in time with my feet

as they slap the gravel.
Pound, pound, pound.
Slap, slap, slap.

I reach the only paved road in our village,
the one where we need to stop and look
before crossing,
but there's no stopping me.
It's only the angry *tring tring!*
of a bicycle bell
that makes me freeze midway.
Luckily, it's just Sunil,
who is by my side in a flash,
bike flung to the ground.

I must look horrific.
My hair whips with the wind,
the ties long lost,
and my face feels
grubby and smudgy and wet.
Tears.
Lots of them.

He doesn't ask.
He sits me down on the concrete bund
that borders the road.
Gravel on one side,
paddy field on the other.

We face the paddy side.
My breath

s l o w s
down
as my eyes scan the
bright green,
light green,
yellow
squares of paddy.

Amma is sending me off
to a school in Colombo
to live with Mala Nanda
and I thought she would come but . . .
my voice trails off.
I can't bring myself to say it,
to accept what seems like a
gross distortion of my life.
but there's a big TV in the new place,
I finish unconvincingly.

What I don't say is that
Amma has a new family that needs her here,
that the last thing she obviously wants is me—
the only remnant of
the life she plans to forget.

Moving forward

Sunil refuses to let me wallow.
He drags me to the tea shop nearby.
We weave through the bananas

hanging in bunches at the entrance,
our faces bumping against
bright green,
light green,
yellow
bananas.

I am greeted by the tea shop regulars.
They clap me on my back and congratulate me.
News travels fast around here.
Cake on the house for our golden girl!
the tea shop aunty announces.
My tummy growls as she places
a cup of extra-sweet tea in front of me
and a generous slice of crumbly butter cake
complete with a fly already honing in.
I am reminded that I haven't eaten anything
since breakfast.

I break the piece of cake into two,
pass one half to Sunil.
We nibble at it bit by bit
and when we're done
we pick the crumbs off the plates with our fingers
and lick those too.

Feeling better? Sunil asks,
his eyes twinkling.

I do.

The messenger

An army officer walks in
and sits at the table right next to us,
the one with the carrom board.
Sunil abandons me without hesitation
and hovers near the officer
who invites him to play.
Sunil takes his seat opposite,
his chest puffed with pride.
He idolizes soldiers.
Also, he loves carrom.

They start to play.
I pluck a banana and settle to watch.
The officer smiles at me.
I blush furiously and take a slurp of my tea.
Men in uniform are aplenty around here,
but they still scare me.
I've heard what happens on the battlefield.
How the uniform turns all these smiling people
into robots who follow commands
and cannot show mercy.

It was different with Thaththa,
who I hardly saw in his uniform,
which was saved for
hellos and goodbyes
and, finally,
the casket.

Another villager stops to congratulate me.
What are they congratulating you for?
the officer asks me
between bites of his cake.
He got it free too.
Army officers are treated
like demigods around here.

She came first in the ENTIRE district
in the scholarship exam,
Sunil interrupts before I can answer.
He's such a suck-up sometimes.
The officer's eyebrows shoot up.
What a wonderful achievement for
such a little girl. You must be so happy.
It's a good thing my mouth is full of banana
so I don't have to respond.

She can even go to Colombo!
Imagine that!
Sunil. Again.
If he was closer, I'd pinch him.

I haven't even decided yet.
Maybe I'm hoping for Amma to
have a miraculous change of heart
by the time I get home.

Have you been to Colombo, officer?
I heard that you can see the ocean when you go there.
Have you seen the ocean?

Sunil is still talking,
but the officer is looking at me.
I almost look away,
but his eyes are so warm and caring
that, for a moment,
his face is replaced by my father's,
and a comforting warmth
spreads through me.
So when the officer speaks,
it's as if it's really my father
reaching out to me from beyond, saying,
Not many get this opportunity.
Take it!
And good luck.

So that's what I decide to do.

Too late

I keep
hoping,
wishing,
praying
that things
might still work out.
But if there's one thing that's hard to change,
it's a baby growing in your stomach.

As the new year approaches,
and with it, my imminent departure,
my hope grows

smaller,
smaller,
smaller
as the baby grows
bigger,
bigger,
bigger.

It's too late.
Too late for Amma.
Too late for me.

Hard

I may be leaving,
but I make sure I don't go
without a fight.

This time I don't
cry,
scream,
or make a fuss.
I shut up
and shut down,
not even wishing Amma
a happy new year.
Why should I
when all she's done is
make mine sad?

Soft

Amma's tummy is still taut,
but there is something about her
that has become
soft.

She cries because I'm going,
and that's a sign if there ever was one.
It's probably more a sign of guilt
than a sign of love,
although I like to think
it's the latter.

She cries while she packs my bag,
when we go to the temple for blessings,
and I hear her cry at night too from behind the curtain.
I could have asked her then,
Why don't you want me?
When did you stop loving me?
but I don't want to.
I don't know how to.

She cries all the way to the bus stop where,
to add insult to injury,
she is sending me to Colombo with Siripala.
The doctor doesn't want her to travel long distances.
Something about her age and being pregnant.
That's why you should act your age,
I had snapped when she told me the night before,
enjoying seeing her eyes well up.
Making her cry made me feel powerful,

although I sensed the eyes
of our Buddha statue at home
reprimanding me.
It was he who proclaimed the mother
as the Buddha-at-home.
Well, if she isn't acting like one,
then I don't have to treat her like one,
I silently debated with him.

But as we wait for our bus,
necks craning each time we see one in the distance,
ready to pounce the minute it arrives
so that we can grab a good seat,
my legs get heavier and heavier
as if I'm growing roots
and I have to stare at the sky every few seconds
to stop the tears from leaking.
Look who is a statue now!

The bus creeps up,
shudders to a stop, and I—
in a move I've practiced multiple times—
put on my backpack and climb the footboard
in one swift move,
no looking back,
as if I don't care that I am
leaving her.

It must be all those Hindi movies I watch
that's made me such a good
actress.

BIGGER AND BETTER

COLOMBO, SRI LANKA, JANUARY 1998

The big city

A voice calls out over the speakers,
You have arrived at the Colombo Fort bus station.
Please take all of your belongings!
Do not leave any unattended bags!
Unattended bags
mean panic, fear,
and the bomb squad.
We make sure to take all our bags.

It's raining.
Raining outside
as well as inside:
leaking through the bus stand ceiling,
dripping from folded umbrellas,
muddying the already dirty floor,
staining my new shoes.
There's litter on the ground,
bodies pressed together,
and lots of strange smells,
and I don't mean that in a good way.

I swallow my disappointment.
This isn't
fresh,

different,
exciting.

I try to stay close to Siripala,
walking as fast as I can,
afraid I'll get lost.
He waits for me to catch up
and offers me his hand.
I don't want to take it.
Luckily,
I don't have to,
because just then
we are pushed by the crowd
and spat out onto the sidewalk.

Colombo,
here I am.

First glimpse

Mala Nanda is waving at us,
standing under an umbrella,
grinning.
So different to how she looked
when I saw her last
at the funeral.

Ah, Siripala aiya, how are you?
The journey must have been very tiring.
She doesn't wait for us to answer

and beckons to us to hurry up.
We squeeze into the waiting tuk-tuk.

There are no doors,
just a transparent flap to keep
the downpour out.
The traffic lights blur in the rain,
shining splotches
on faded plastic.
I peer over the tuk driver's shoulder
for a better look through the windscreen
and catch my first glimpse of the city.

Row after row of concrete buildings,
each with multiple floors
that reach up to the sky.
They are draped with strings of twinkling lights.
Leftovers of Christmas and new year festivities,
Mala Nanda says,
pointing with her chin.
*What's there to celebrate when
so many are dying?* she adds.
I ignore her negativity.

It's good to celebrate
what you can,
when you can,
while you can.

Mala Nanda

is my mother's Akka—
her older sister.

She left the village when she was a teenager
to work as a housemaid
in one of the big Colombo homes.
*Too many mouths to feed
and not much to feed them with,*
Amma said
when I asked why someone
would send their child away.

It seems village folk
have many reasons
to send their kids away.
Reasons that wouldn't exist
if they were
rich.

Checkpoints and soldiers

dot the sides of the roads,
stopping vehicles,
asking for identification.
So many more
than back home.
I count at least fifteen.

If they have got a tip-off,
they stop all vehicles matching the description.
And they also check for suspicious people,
Mala Nanda explains.
By suspicious people
she actually means
suspicious Tamil people.
They are there to protect us.

If they are there to keep us safe,
why does it make me feel so
unsafe?

Hunger

At the traffic lights,
street vendors sell
cashew,
vadai,
fried gram,
pickled mango.
Mala Nanda extends a hand with some money out
and in comes a greasy little paper bag
made of old magazine pages.
You must be hungry, she says
handing it to us.

The bag is warm,
the vadai inside warmer.
Coconut-oil-fried,

crunchy, munchy,
golden balls of lentils.
In a few bites
my share is gone,
gobbled up greedily.
Now that I have arrived,
I am suddenly hungry for whatever
this city has to offer.

Being rich

This is what being rich means,
according to me:

Being rich means you can eat
whatever you want
whenever you want it,
even things like ice cream,
because you need to be rich
to own a fridge.
(We once bought a small fridge with our savings,
but then we couldn't afford the
electricity bill.)

Being rich also means a big house
with more than one room,
and a car.
I've never been in a car.
They must have one where we're staying.
I hope I'll get to go in it.

Being rich also means that
you get to do exactly what you want.

No need to hope,
no need to wait,
and no need to choose.

Still

Mala Nanda is not a teenager anymore—
far from it—
but she looks good.
Her slippers aren't worn,
her teeth are white and unstained,
and there's a small tummy roll above her waistline,
which means she is well-fed.

But she's still a housemaid
at the same house
working for the same people.

You'd think after all those years of working
she'd have her own house and car too.

They're still rich.
She's still not rich enough.

A way out

She had her "way out" once.

She had gotten married—
eloped with the driver
who worked for her mistress.
But her husband was apparently a
good-for-nothing alcoholic
and disappeared long ago.
Whenever my mother speaks of him
she actually spits: *Thoo!*
The ultimate denouncement.

It would have been better if she had
never gotten married,
Amma says.
Which is surprising,
since she herself couldn't wait
to find a new husband.

Big gates, big doors

So big that the vadai inside my tummy
are doing their own juggling act.
We are here at what will be
my new home.
I clutch at the thin gold chain around my neck
and follow Mala Nanda inside,
wondering what's in store for me.

The Palace

My eyes aren't big enough to capture it all
and my brain turns to mush.

This is a palace!

It's tall,
white,
inviting
with huge windows,
winding stairways,
and—I blink fast—
a swimming pool!
I thought they only had those in the movies.
There are also not one but
TWO cars.

Even the family who owns the palace
—the King, the Queen, and the Princess—
seem perfect.
Smiling, happy, beautiful.

My aunt is clearly
the lowly handmaiden,
and I'll obviously be the
handmaiden's helper.

But who cares?

I'm living in a palace!

Thank you and goodbye

It is said that when Sri Lankans
say goodbye
they don't really mean it.

They say goodbye once
and start chatting again,
then they say goodbye once more
and the chatting continues.
On repeat.

Siripala is packed and ready to go,
and Mala Nanda's Sri Lankan goodbye
is in full force.
I mean, the man has a bus to catch
but she keeps on yakking,
glancing at me
every few minutes.

I know that they're talking about me.
I hate that they're talking about me.

When Siripala finally comes over
to say goodbye to me,
I wave so quickly that
one might think
I'm not Sri Lankan.

He presses a crumpled note into my hand.
A whole five hundred rupees.

This is for you.
Thunuruwan saranai.
As if to say,
Thanks for disappearing.
Here's some money for your efforts.
Paying me off.

I raise my eyes to meet his,
hoping he'll see my disdain,
but he only smiles.
The fool.

I consider refusing the money
but I want to be rich someday.
Bribe money is not the best way to start
but I'll take it.

Unfamiliar

I wake up at dawn
and then lie back down,
unsure of what to do.

The house is pin-drop silent,
only broken by the faraway melody
of the bread van making its rounds.

My nose is lonely.
It misses the sweet scent of jasmine,
the comforting aroma of ginger brewing in the tea,

the sharp smell of fresh manure from the cows outside.

It misses home.

Garage access

Our bedroom is on the ground floor.
It's almost as big as my entire house
back in the village.
And the best part?
It's right next to the garage!

My sleep was full of wild dreams
in which I was being driven about in fancy cars,
even the es-yoo-vee,
which is what the funny-shaped enormous one is called.

I can't wait for Mala Nanda to
wake up and show me around
but her snores tell me
it won't be for a while.
I slide off the bed
and open the door quietly.

And there they are,
both in a row.
Metal bodies
and massive wheels.
Gleaming,
glorious.

I sit on the doorstep
and stare
and stare.

The King and the Queen

or rather,
the Madam and the Sir,
are super nice.

I can't stop staring at Madam.
She's not as pretty as Amma
but she is dressed so nicely.
Her fingers with the
bright red nails and glittery rings
constantly push her long hair back.
She wears it loose,
flowing over her shoulders.
My hands itch to tie it.

Sir is tall, very tall,
and he has the widest smile.
He's dressed nicely too.
His shirt looks new
and so do his pants,
and nothing is too small
or too big.
A perfect fit.

Looks like being rich
means you can also
be well-dressed.

They ask about
my life back home,
my future school,
and what I want to be,
and don't laugh when I say
I want to be
a lawyer.

Sir switches on the AC as we talk.
Beep.
The AC is a white box that makes a room cold.
So cold that bumps appear on my arms
and my teeth start to chatter.
Embarrassing!

I'm glad when the Princess arrives.
She takes me by the hand
and rescues me.

Sasha

is the Princess's name.

She looks just like the
girl model in the poster
in our village barber shop.

Fair like a foreigner,
hair in a short bob,
and an Alice band
to keep the fringe
away from her eyes.
She gives me a tour of the house
while I try not to look at her legs
in shorts so short
it makes me blush.

I call her Podi Madam—
small madam—
even though she is older than me
by three years.
But she shakes her head when I say it.
Just call me Sasha.

In her room,
she lets me sit on her bed
as she shows me all her Barbie dolls.
I don't play with them anymore.
You can have them if you want.

I've never seen a Barbie doll before.
They are hideous,
stick thin with hard pointy breasts.
No wonder she doesn't play with them.
But I don't tell her that.

I'm too caught up in the
luxury that surrounds me.

Her bedsheets are soft and silky,
the pillows are like fluffy clouds,
and their smell—
no, their scent—
is of flowers and fresh rain.

Heavenly.

The lowdown

Mala Nanda fills me in
on how things work around here.

Sir is an architect.
He has his own firm and works so hard
he's almost never at home,
poor thing.

Sasha is a lovely child.
Like you, Kavi,
Mala Nanda says,
her face lighting up.
She's given everything she asks for.
A little . . . spoilt.
Not like me at all then.

Madam is . . .
pause
nice.
Her voice drops to a whisper.

She can't cook.
It's a good thing I'm here.
If not, who would cook Sir's favorite food?
Mala Nanda has been cooking for Sir
since he was around my age.

They adore her.
I see it in the way they thank her for the food she cooks,
the way they look her in the eye when asking for help,
the way they've made room for me
because of her.

I don't blame her for sticking around.
It's nice to be around people who
treat you so well.

New school

Mala Nanda and I trail behind
the principal who's showing us around
my new school.
She wanted to talk to us before
I officially start
tomorrow.

I watch her plump body,
swathed in a bright blue sari,
swaying as she walks.
Left, right,
left, right.

She fills the space with her perfume
and the strong smell tickles my nose.

I'm not as anxious as I thought I would be.
It helps that it's a Sunday
and that the school is
practically empty.
Maybe it's the emptiness
that makes it look bigger than it is.
I've never seen such long corridors
or such large gardens.
Or maybe it really is
this big.

Everything fascinates me,
even the washrooms
that have tiled walls and cubicles
and, get this, actual commodes!
My old school just had a hole in the ground.
So did our toilet at home.
I hadn't even sat on an actual commode
till I came to Colombo.

We are shown the
gymnasium—a place you exercise,
auditorium—a huge room with a stage,
tennis court—a green rectangle where
you play a sport called tennis,
and swimming pool—
that one I knew!
And every time

the principal says the same thing:
I'm sure you may not have seen this
in your village . . .

I want to tell her
if we had all this in my village
then I wouldn't have had to
leave everything to be here.
Instead,
I open my eyes wide in awe
to show her
how grateful I am.

Finally, she takes us into a large room
and sits behind a large desk
that's in front of a large display
of trophies and medals.
She speaks for a long time,
saying important things, I bet.
Mala Nanda nods a lot
and I do too, although
I have no idea of what I am nodding to.

I can only stare at her mouth.
Her lips are painted blood red.
She's not a good painter
because there is a smear of lipstick on her front teeth.
So distracting.

When she smiles—
a bit too widely—

I see her extra-pointy canines.
It makes her look
like a friendly vampire.

Later, those toothy smiles
would become actual fangs bared,
but today she is just a person
with sharp, stained teeth.

The first day

Mala Nanda drops me off at the gate,
pats the pleats of my uniform one last time,
centers my tie that's weighed down
by a shiny metal school badge,
and rearranges my two plaits
so they rest on my chest.

I did my hair by myself,
leaving out the ribbons Amma gave me
on purpose.

There is an army checkpoint at the entrance
and security to check inside our bags
in case one of us might be carrying a bomb.
I remember Thaththa and feel a pang in my chest,
and for a moment
I wish things were different.

Then I join the sea of children
and their noisy chatter reminds me
of where I am going,
making me forget
where I'm coming from.

Fitting in

I am supposed to go to 6A
but all I can see is a row of 7s.
I circle the building, lost,
and find myself near the 8s.
A flurry of panic rises up in my chest,
pushed back down when a
kind-looking akka comes to my rescue,
pointing me in the right direction.
The classrooms over here
don't just go next to each other:
they go above each other as well.

I find my class upstairs and walk in,
then pause when I notice that
no one notices me.
I see an empty desk right at the back
and take my seat in a row of girls
who look as lost as I feel.
They must be the other scholarship kids.

I hope I don't look too nervous.
I arrange my face into
what I think is a friendly smile.

But they don't smile back
and my cheeks start to hurt after a while
and I give up.

Happy, fearless, popular

That's when I see the two of them,
sitting to the front and right of me.

They have smooth skin,
shiny hair tied in ponytails
that bob up and down as they talk,
and clean, pink fingernails.
Their school bags aren't the standard plain ones,
but have foreign cartoon characters on them
and fancy zips that open to reveal
books adorned with the prettiest stickers.
They aren't huddled together,
talking in whispers.
Their voices are crisp,
their laughter loud and unafraid,
not caring that the rest of the students
keep glancing at them
with both annoyance
and envy.

I want to be friends with these
happy,
fearless,
popular

girls
who look like they
belong.

So I could also be
happy,
fearless,
popular
and maybe even
belong.

Too different

I look down at my arms,
covered in scars where I've scratched at mosquito bites,
and at my fingernails crusted with soil
left over from when I potted plants with Mala Nanda.
I realize I'm
too different,
too not-enough,
for them to ever
want to be friends
with me.

Not that different

Around me the chatter continues.
Some discuss their holidays,
some compare their new books,

and then I hear someone mention
Shah Rukh Khan.

My ears prick up at the mention of
my Hindi movie star idol.
It's coming from the duo,
giggling and looking down.
I crane my neck till I see what they're looking at—
a bunch of postcards from which the faces
of my favorite Bollywood stars smile at me.
I asked my mother if I could hang up his posters
in my room and she said yes!
She even gave me money to buy one.

I perk up when I hear this.
At home, in the space next to my bed,
hang a few postcards of some of my own favorites—
Madhuri Dixit, Rani Mukherjee, Aamir Khan—
bought after much agonizing
about who was worth spending
my birthday present money on.
But among them, one stands out,
life-size and lifelike.
Shah Rukh Khan,
smiling down at me
from the largest poster I could find.

Maybe I'm not that different
after all.

Not yet

Sasha wants to know if I've made any friends.
I tell her,
Not yet.
I tell her,
Soon.

It's been a week
and I'm still trying
to be noticed;
to be seen.

Invisible

In the village I was
the smart one,
the popular one,
the admired one.

In the city I am
the new one,
the poor one,
the invisible one.

Sasha says

Sasha must have loads of friends
because she knows all about making them

and she shares all this knowledge with me.
She gives me pointers
on what looks too eager
and what looks
not eager enough.

I hang on her every word
refusing to be distracted.
Being myself isn't enough anymore.
Even Amma thought so—
so why wouldn't these strangers?
If I want to be their friend,
I will have to change.

It's time for a new me.

Bad influence

I don't have to look too anything
to be friends with Sasha.
She seems to like my company.

I wonder why her friends don't come over.
Who wouldn't want to play with all these toys?
Or take a dip in the swimming pool out back?
I'm curious. I ask her.
Their parents think I'm a bad influence.
Anyway, I like being alone.

I don't believe her.

While I actually enjoy being alone,
Sasha seems to avoid it at all costs.
I can tell by the way she makes me
hang out with her every evening.
By the way she asks me to stay
a little bit longer
when I need to go.

And why would her influence
ever be considered bad?
I love her influence!
I think it's great!

Not what it seems

Mala Nanda explains.
Remember I said Sasha is spoilt?
It means she gets away with anything.
And the more she does,
the more she keeps doing it, as if
she wants to see when her parents will snap.
Sometimes I worry she won't stop
till she gets into big trouble.
That, or till her parents show her
they love her.

I am no less confused.
Nothing is what it seems
and it's giving me a headache.
But, Mala Nanda,

isn't it good that your parents
don't find fault with you?
Isn't that love?

Mala Nanda ruffles my hair.
Oh, Kavi, you have a lot to learn about love.

And life,
she adds as an afterthought.

Like I said,
no less confused.

Practice makes perfect

I practice my can-I-be-your-friend face
in the mirror
as I replay Sasha's advice in my head.
Don't look interested.
Just be interesting.

I don't think there is a
whole lot interesting about me,
but I am interested
in everything.

Yes, but don't show them that.
Sasha says this is how to be cool.
Seems like there is more to it

than getting used to
all the air conditioning in the house.

Practice makes friends

All the training on Sasha's part
and practicing on my part
finally pays off.

At the end of my second week,
I am humming a popular Shah Rukh Khan song
just loud enough to be heard
by the cool kids
when one of them turns to me and asks,
Do you like him too?

Yes.
Yes, I like him VERY MUCH.
Be cool, Kavi.
Not too eager, remember.

Especially in Dil to Pagal Hai,
I add and look away.
Interesting,
not interested.

Nethmi

I know her name
(everyone does),
although I know she doesn't know mine.

Where did you see that?
She looks surprised but tries to hide it
as she scratches at the peeling nail polish
on her fingernails.
Nail polish that isn't allowed in school.
I wish I was that brave.

In the cinema, I answer proudly.
Madam and Sir had taken all of us to watch it over the weekend.
Shah Rukh and Madhuri filled the screen,
larger than life.
Just like everything in this city.

Sulo

The girl next to Nethmi
scrapes her chair back,
swings around,
her face alive.

Madhuri is sooo gorgeous, isn't she?
My mother says I look like her,
but since when does Madhuri wear glasses?

She grins at me.
I'm Sulo.

I'm about to say that I agree
with her mother
when I'm interrupted.
And since when is Madhuri so dark?
Nethmi's laugh is tinkly.
Sulo's face falls.

Nethmi laughs harder.
She is looking at me like
she wants me to laugh with her.

So I do.

Broken English

I am able to swap seats with the girl
who sits behind Nethmi and Sulo.
My persistence pays off,
and they start slowly including me
in their conversations.

I often have to listen extra closely
whenever they speak.
If I don't, I risk not understanding
and losing track entirely.
They switch between English and Sinhala often.

Sasha says this is called "Singlish"
and is a sign of being cool.

Until now, I've only spoken in Sinhala.
I don't know much English.
And what I do know is apparently called
"Broken English,"
which basically means that
the English I speak is incorrect.
Broken.

It's not *My name Kavi*
it's *My name is Kavi*
or, *I am Kavi*,
and I need to leave out the part
where I pound on my chest
to indicate myself.

Actually, I tell Sasha proudly one day,
*my full name according to my birth certificate is
Senasinghe Mudiyanselage Aruni Kavindya Bandara.*
Sasha fills her cheeks with air
and lets it out in a whoosh.
Err, no.
Just call yourself Kavi.
We're trying to make you cool, remember?

There is so much to learn.
And until I do,
maybe it's safer to
just listen.

Topics of conversation

In the village, everything anyone
thinks about,
talks about,
dreads,
looks forward to,
is somehow connected
to the war.

Over here,
people have other things to
think about,
talk about,
dread,
look forward to.

What they talk about

Parents.
Houses.
Cars.
Servants.
Dogs.
Cats.

The Weekly Top 40.
The Backstreet Boys.
Leo & Kate.
Mandira Bedi.

After-school sports practices.
Hockey.
Swimming.
Piano lessons.
Cricket.
Boys' schools.
Homework.

The latest bomb.
Who died.
Who didn't die.
And who is left
with what lifelong disability
because of it.

My turn

Sulo is usually a chatterbox
but she's quiet today
recovering from a bout of flu.
So I guess I should have been prepared
for the void her chattering left.
I should have known what to say
when their faces suddenly settle on me
and Nethmi's sharp voice cuts through the silence to ask
the question they hadn't thought to ask
all this while.

Kavi, what's new with you?

Pansil

are the five precepts in Buddhism—
the basic things a good Buddhist must do.

Not killing,
not stealing,
not kissing and hugging lots of people at the same time,
not lying,
not drinking alcohol.

It's important to follow these precepts
if you want to be a good person,
and you can follow this advice
even if you aren't a Buddhist.

Like Madam and Sir.
They are Christians
but they are good people.
Even though I've seen them
drink alcohol sometimes.
They call them cocktails.

I've always been good too.
Well, except for squishing ants,
killing mosquitos,
or that one time I took a sip of toddy
that Amma had left to ferment.
(It was horrible. Served me right.)

But when I answer Nethmi's question,

I lie.

A bad Buddhist

Not a small lie either,
like how I didn't do my homework
because I had a headache,
when in reality it was because
I had helped Ranjith wash the cars.

Today's lie was a big lie.
A very big lie.

And I know this makes me
a bad person,
but if I had to
I would do it
all over again.

OLD HOUSE, NEW PAINT

The challenge

It doesn't come out without a fight.
The lie I mean.

First, it forms itself into a ball
and lodges itself halfway in my throat.
I cough it up
and as it lies there on my tongue,
a hundred different scenarios
play like a reel in my mind.

They're waiting for my answer.
Sulo's eyes are wide and curious.
Nethmi's eyebrows are raised.
I don't like it when
people raise their eyebrows like that.
It means they think you
can't do something.

That raised eyebrow is a challenge.
I never back down from a challenge.

I pause the reel
and open my mouth.

They into We

Ah, nothing much.
We got—
My throat seizes up again.
Geez, talk about timing!
I take a big gulp.
We got a new car! I say,
the same way I would announce to the villagers
that our cow had birthed a calf.
At least this lie is based on some truth.
Sir had driven home yesterday in a
car with only two doors.
The most beautiful car I've ever seen!

Nethmi's eyebrows are still raised.
What is it?

It's yellow with a black roof
that goes down with a button!
My arm becomes the roof.
I wave it to and fro to show them.
Prrrrt! Prrrrt! I add sound effects.
Sulo giggles.

No, I mean what is the make?
Nethmi again.
Why does she sound so disbelieving?
Ugh!

Is it a BMW?
Sulo is trying to guess,
as was I.

Yes, yes that's the one!
I am relieved that she guesses it for me.
I had forgotten what the
upside-down M was called.

Sulo squeals.
That's the latest one!
My thaththa has been talking about it all the time!
It's nice to see her so thrilled over what I say
for a change.

I peek at Nethmi.
Her eyebrows
are lowered.

The bell rings and
I walk back to my seat,
heart still pounding.

I think they believed me.
And all I had to do
was turn the
"they"
into
"we."

This is me

My parents live in the biggest house in the village.
My mother runs the family business
and my father is a big shot in the army
with lots of medals.

My mother cried and didn't want me to leave
but she knows my future has bigger things in it
and that the city is where I'll be able
to make all my—and their—
dreams come true.
She calls me every day
because that's how much she misses me,
but I tell her to hold on and be strong.

I live with my aunt, uncle,
and cousin Sasha
and they love me
as if I'm their own.

They buy me anything I want
and let me eat anything I like,
even the cornflakes that are kept
on the highest shelves where the
food from other countries is stored.
And we have two vehicles—
a car, an es-yoo-vee,
and now the BMW.

Oh yeah.

That makes it
three vehicles.

Better this way

Mala Nanda insists I talk to Amma
once a week,
using the telephone
with permission from Madam.

Sometimes I air-dial the numbers
and have pretend conversations.
It's better this way, I tell myself.
She doesn't have to bother with me anymore.
Soon she'll have a new child,
one that will bring her
all the happiness
I never did.

I choose to write letters instead.
Writing is easier than talking
and I want her to know I'm moving on too.
I tell her how amazing my new home is,
how nice Madam and Sir are,
and how Sasha plays with me
and lets me sit on her bed.

Amma writes back to me saying that
I must have done something really good in my past
to deserve all this.

I write back telling her
that if I was really that good
she would be here with me.

Then I crush it and toss it in the bin.

Ever since I lied

Nethmi and Sulo seem friendlier.
Soon, I am part of their clique.

It's like I was always there.
They won't even go outside without me.
Kavi, are you coming? They'll call out to me
when the bell rings for recess,
making sure I'm with them
as they make their way to the far end
of the enormous school ground
to their spot.
I guess you could call it
our spot now.

There is no kohomba tree here
but there is a madatiya tree,
its long branches sheltering us
while we sit on the grass,
separating the hard, shiny red seeds
from their curly brown pods.
I fill up my pockets with the madatiya seeds
that Nethmi and Sulo absentmindedly pass to me

while they
chat
chat
chat
nonstop.

I don't have much to add.
Apart from supporting the same side in the war
and loving Bollywood movies,
all I have in common with my new friends
are all the things I do with Sasha and her parents.
All the things that
people who have lots of money do.

Like having a gardener who comes in weekly,
or handing out money to the beggars near the traffic lights,
or whipping out a card to pay the bill at the supermarket.
The bill that has so many zeroes at the end
I have to count them aloud to believe it.

Back home, Amma needs to
tend to the vegetables for months—
turning the soil,
watching for insects,
watering them through the drought—
and it's only then that she earns
what rich people spend
on a week's groceries.

Shopping with Madam

When I'm not jealously wishing
that Amma and I had a magic card that paid our bills,
I actually enjoy grocery shopping with Madam.

She pushes the cart,
tapping her bright red nails on the handle,
her glittery rings reflecting the overhead lights
as she sashays down the aisles
saying things like,
Kavi, did you get the milk powder?
Kavi, what else did Mala need?

It makes me feel so important.
I take extra care selecting the vegetables,
breaking the tips of the okra to make sure they're fresh,
shaking the coconuts till I hear the water sloshing inside.

Afterward,
I sit with Madam in the back of the car,
the seat cushioning my bony limbs,
while Ranjith drives us.
Madam never lets Sasha sit in the front
when Ranjith is driving.
It is one of those things that are
Not Done.

I like how she never lets me
sit in the front either.

Bulletproof

Honk!
Honk!
Hoooooonnnnkkk!

It's as if someone's hand
has got stuck to their horn.
We are being chased off the road.

Whizz!
Whizz!
Whizz!

Soldiers on motorbikes
race in front,
point their rifles,
ask us to

Move!
Move!
Move!

My heart thuds.

We're being attacked.

I slide off the seat,
crouch and huddle.

Kavi, get up. Don't worry.
It's just some politician.
Look!
Madam says
pointing out the window.
She does this when she's showing me
something rare and interesting
like a bullock cart
or an elephant,
things I see in the village
almost daily.

I creep up to see
a massive car speed past,
black with black windows.
More soldiers on motorbikes
following it.

It's bulletproof, she whispers
as if I should be impressed.

I'm not.
I guess being scared out of your wits
while almost crashing into the cars around you
is something I'll have to get used to
in this city.

Ambulthiyal fish

As the weeks pass,
I start finding my voice.

Nethmi and Sulo's
unsuspecting acceptance of me
gives me confidence
and I settle into my new role
with surprising ease.

I tell them about how, back home,
I help my mother cook breakfast,
marinading the fish in a clay pot
for her famous ambulthiyal preparation.
How my father wakes me up at the crack of dawn
to go to the fish market
for the freshest catch of the day.
And how we all wait,
mouths watering and stomachs growling,
till the food is served and we can heap
steaming hot kiribath onto our plates,
drenching the milk rice in fish gravy,
and digging into it with our fingers.

I notice my friends swallowing spit as they listen,
which is understandable
because I do too.

Based on a true story

That story is a real one.
It's one of my favorite memories.

I find myself talking more about my own family
even though I'm acting
as if they don't exist.

It helps the words come out faster
when some of what I say is true.
It's like the same old house
with a new coat of paint.

Or in my case,
the same old house
with some major renovations.

Not that simple

It's Madam's idea to have Ranjith pick me up
every day after school
because my school is on the way to Sasha's.
It's safer than taking the bus, she says.

Ranjith and I chat about anything
and everything.
He's like a big brother to me.

There's a picture on the dashboard
that wasn't there before.
Who is that?
Some actress you like?
I tease him.
This is the girl I'm marrying,
he says, passing it to me.

In it, a girl gives an almost-smile
where her lips are pressed together
but you know there's a huge tooth-baring grin
waiting just beneath.
On her forehead, in between her eyebrows
is a small black dot.
A pottu.

She's Tamil,
Ranjith tells me,
though I had guessed the minute I saw the pottu.
It's what all Tamil women wear in Sri Lanka.
Or rather, used to wear.
I overheard Mala Nanda and Ranjith discussing it once.
With the war, wearing the pottu became unsafe—
a reason to be
stared at,
singled out,
suspected.

Ranjith sighs the deepest sigh.
He says his parents don't approve.
And neither do her parents.
A Sinhalese and a Tamil falling in love
is a big no-no.

So what will you do?

We'll wait for them to change their minds,
but if they don't . . .
His voice trails off.

You'll elope?
I ask, excited.

Ranjith looks sad.
It's not that simple.

But it is,
I want to say.
Leaving everything behind
and starting anew is
very simple.

Just like that

Sasha goes to a private Catholic school
with stern-looking nuns
who are constantly confiscating her
glitter shoelaces,
glitter hairbands,
glitter nail polish,
and complaining about it to Madam and Sir
every chance they get.

I'm glad I don't go there,
even though I wonder why Sasha can't just
follow the rules.

Ranjith parks the car outside the school.
The door opens and
Sasha climbs in,
flinging her bag onto my lap,
her long legs pushing mine aside.

Hi, Ranjith!
Hi, Kavi!
she chirps cheerfully,
and the mood in the car changes
just like that.

Untouched

Sasha lives a life
untouched by the worries
that muddy the waters of the minds
of those like Ranjith
and me.

No death,
no distance,
no discrimination,
no drama.

She is a lotus
risen above all the muck.

It gives me hope
that a different life
is possible.

Good days

Some days are better
than others.

Like when I score the highest points
on the weekly surprise quiz,
or when I'm selected for the school track team,
beating Nethmi whose mouth puckered
as if she were sucking on a lime.
Or when Ranjith picks me up after school
and I get in like I've been doing it all my life,
pressing the button that makes the window whir down
so I can wave bye to my friends.
The window whirs back up again at my command.
I lean back and wonder at
how easy it is to be happy
when you are
rich.

Hard days

are when Nethmi and Sulo
ask me for books to swap with theirs.

Although we speak mostly in Sinhala,
or rather Singlish,
they prefer reading books written in English
by authors with foreign names
and white kids on the covers
who look nothing like us.

I don't have any books like that and
I don't show too much interest
in case they find out
that I can't read English as well as they do.
So they just assume that I'm
not a reader.

They needn't know
that I own a closely guarded stack of
classic Sinhala novels,
collected over the years,
including those by famous Sri Lankan authors
like Martin Wickramasinghe
and T. B. Ilangaratne,
as well as translations from the Soviet Union.

They don't know
how I taught myself to read
(because Amma didn't teach me

and Thaththa was never around);
how I can finish a book in a day.

They don't know
that I have pages and pages of letters
folded under my pillowcase,
read so many times
I know them by heart.

10:1

The letters are from Thaththa to me,
sent while he was away on duty.
There are also letters from Amma
sent during these past few months.

The ratio is around 10:1.
It's not surprising
that I still get more attention
from my dead father
than from my mother
who is very much alive.

The worst day

is when Nethmi invites the whole class
to a party at the new amusement park
for her birthday.

I badly want to go
but I don't have anything to wear
or anything that I can give her as a gift.

Not that she would have guessed it
by the way I clap and cheer and tell her
that I bet it will be the best birthday party
I've ever been to.

Which is true because
I've never been
to a birthday party before.

Uniform

That evening,
my homework lies undone next to me.
I'm wondering what to do
about the party.

So far no one has suspected me.
There is no real reason to.
At school we are all
(mostly) equal.
Same uniform,
same rules,
same socks,
same shoes.

I don't have a wristwatch
like most of the others
and my earrings aren't real gold because
Amma had to pawn the real pair for money.
But luckily, no one notices
the small things
when there are two thousand girls
dressed alike.

Clothes: old vs. new

I take out all the clothes I own.
The ones Amma bought brand-new for me
to take to the city.

I still remember how she
pulled each item out of the shopping bag,
watching my reactions.
Like she cared that I liked
what she had picked.

I did,
although it was more because
of the fact that she cared
than the clothes
themselves.

I lay them all out on the bed now.
Five skirts—all knee-length, all bright colored;
three tops—two have Hello Kitty on them,

the other is a *Titanic* T-shirt;
and two dresses—one with a big collar
and a bow at the back,
the other a plain white one to wear to temple.

None of these seem suitable for a party,
not even the one with a big collar and bow,
although that is the
dressiest of the lot.
Not for *this* party
anyway.

None of these
are like anything
Sasha or the girls on English TV
wear.

Something tells me
that these clothes,
the ones the old me would wear,
should not be the clothes
that the new me wears.

Separate

Gosh, look at you!
If you frown anymore,
I'll have to peel your forehead apart
to find your face!
Sasha has the funniest way of saying things.

She wants to be a writer someday.
She says that a good writer
needs to find ways to make the ordinary
sound extraordinary.
She does that part pretty well already.

It hurts a bit here.
I touch my chest.

You're having a heart attack?
She looks concerned
but her mouth turns up at the corners.
I almost tell her that my father died of one
and that it's anything but funny,
but I don't want to mix my two worlds together.

Sasha hardly asks and I hardly tell.
I like it this way.

It lets me keep
my worlds separate.
Just like Cinderella.
In one world I'm
a pauper;
in the other,
a princess.

Mixed

Sasha grabs her Discman
(a music player you can carry around)
and sits down next to me,
crossing her legs and popping her earphones in.

She glances at my feet,
takes her earphones out.
Is that a hole in your slipper?
You need new ones.
Sasha is also very blunt sometimes.
She better work on that.

She stands,
walks over to her shoe rack,
tosses a pair of slippers at me.
They're not new.
I've seen her wear them often.
But they're a hundred times nicer
than my plain black pair
and they don't have holes.

She does this often,
this sharing of shoes,
clothes,
food,
toys.

Ah, that's so much better!
Pause.
Why are you still frowning so?

Even though Sasha can be blunt
and her life's challenges involve
convincing her father to buy her a CD
by a group called the Spice Girls,
she is the most generous person I know.

I decide there are some things
I can share with her too.

Everything

I tell her everything.

Another plan

I don't expect Sasha to react the way she does.

Not one *How could you?*
or *Why did you?*
And when she says,
Now what are we going to do?
it isn't in the way adults would say it
after you confess to doing something wrong—
hand on forehead,
gnashing teeth,
like there is no hope left.

The way Sasha says it—
fingers drumming on the carpet and pupils dilated—

it is more an invitation.
Like not only is there a solution
but that the solution is something
exciting.

The energy in the room shifts,
the load on my chest lifts.

The dreamy look in her eyes disappears
and she wiggles her eyebrows at me.

I have a plan.

Borrowing not stealing

I am totally on board.
I mean, why wouldn't I be?
Here I was
feeling bad for pretending
to be her cousin,
when all I had to do all along
was ask.

From that day on
Sasha literally becomes the voice in my ear.
Telling me not only
what to say,
what to do,
but also
what to listen to and watch.

As part of my education,
she even teaches me
the right way to dance.
I didn't think I needed
any tutoring on the subject
but Sasha says that I should save
my Baila moves for village weddings
and not city parties.
We watch music videos on MTV
of scantily dressed women
pouting their lips and
thrusting their hips.
Sasha imitates them perfectly.
It makes her look so much older than she is.

I can't make myself dance like that,
mostly because I'm too distracted wondering
if Madam or Sir will walk in on us.
But they're hardly ever home
and I begin to relax
and enjoy myself.
Hip thrusting and all.

Mannequin

Sasha teaches me
how to dress.
We pore over fashion magazines,
film magazines,
pop music magazines.

For "inspiration" as she calls it,
as if she's a designer.
(Designers are people who
design clothes and outfits,
deciding what looks good
and what doesn't.
Like Goo-chee and Sha-nel.)

Every time she circles an outfit
and then attempts to recreate it on me
I become her mannequin.
Her model.

A model
modern
girl.

Beautiful

When we play dress-up,
standing in front of her large mirror,
I barely recognize myself
in all these fashionable clothes.

My hair is shorter and glossier.
Sasha cut it a few inches
and gave me something called shampoo
to make it soft and shiny.

Tight denim jeans replace
my rumpled skirt
and an oversized jacket conceals
the Hello Kitty on my T-shirt.
It's a good thing the AC is on
so I don't sweat.

She hands me her Discman,
sliding the earphones over my ears.
If only you were popping a bubblegum right now,
the look would be
totally complete!
she shrieks.
I have no idea
what she is on about,
but I like what I see.

I twirl around,
Sasha's reflection next to mine,
admiring myself
just as much as I admire her.

I always thought Sasha was beautiful
and in that moment
I feel beautiful too.

Bending the rules

It's today!
The day of the party!

Make sure you come early, Kavi.
Sulo squeezes my hand goodbye
when we part at the school gate.
And remember to wear the bracelet!
shouts Nethmi.

The three of us have
matching friendship bracelets now.
Nethmi and Sulo had theirs already
but I only got mine recently,
tucked inside the party invitation.

I never remove it, I remind her,
thinking of it hugging my ankle
underneath my sock,
since I don't have a wristwatch
to hide its forbidden presence.

I try to follow the rules
as much as possible.
Breaking them would place
too much attention on me,
and I don't want to risk
all my hard work.
Instead,
I bend them.

Fizzy

Sasha has my outfit all ready.

A purple and pink stripey dress,
which looks amazing
but ends so high above my knees
that it makes me
uncomfortable.

I want to be different
but not that different.

I wear tights under it
amidst complaints from Sasha,
and transparent sandals with a platform heel
that I'm scared might trip me over at any moment.
Sasha says this is how the Spice Girls dress,
which is Sasha-speak for
fashionable.

She ties my hair high up on my head
and divides my long ponytail into loads of tiny plaits.
I whip them from side to side
and we giggle as their ends
slap against my cheeks.

Even Madam is thrilled to see this new me.
She fetches her camera
to take a photograph.

When Mala Nanda sees me
her hand flies up to her mouth in shock.
The bubbles of excitement rising inside me
stop midway—

Then she drops her hand and says,
Look at this little madam!
She is smiling.

—and the bubbles start fizzing furiously
once again.

Lights, camera, action!

The party is a success.
I am a success.

All our classmates are there.
It's so weird to see everyone in regular clothes.
Weird in a nice way.

There's a Ferris wheel,
a merry-go-round,
and best of all,
dodgem cars!
(I would go in them all night if I could.)
There's candy floss,
and ice cream,
and music so loud
it drowns out everything else.

All the kids cast glances at me,
especially when Nethmi calls
me and Sulo to stand next to her
when she cuts her cake.
She feeds us bites off the first slice,
which is what you do with your
closest family and friends.

Everyone claps
and the camera flashes.
Nethmi, Sulo, and I
huddle in a pose
and beam for a picture.

I'm so happy
I could burst.

Spotlight

Something happens to me.
It pulses through my veins,
courses through my body.

It's what happens
when I hear Sunil's laughter
or Nayana teacher's praise.

It's what happens
when I catch that first glimpse of Thaththa
walking home,

his smile dazzling white against his
rough and weathered face.

It's what happens
when Amma kisses the parting of my hair
as she tucks me into bed,
her hand lingering on my cheek
as she looks at me,
with a gaze so tender.

I had almost forgotten this feeling.
This feeling of being
wanted,
admired,
loved.

It's how I used to feel
in my old life
before everything
changed.

Curtain call

As amazing as the evening is,
the cherry on top comes
when it's time to go.

A familiar horn honks
twice in quick succession—
Ranjith's trademark—

and a bright yellow BMW
appears through the park gates.

I take my time saying goodbye,
thanking Nethmi and her parents,
giving Ranjith time to drive
right up to where the party is.
Right up to me.

It's started to rain,
a soft drizzle.
The flashing lights of the park
reflect on the car's freshly waxed body.
It shimmers and gleams,
wipers gliding soundlessly across its
spotless windscreen.
The effect is mesmerizing.
Nethmi has forgotten
not to look interested.
Next to me, Sulo whispers,
Wow.

It is the perfect end
to the perfect day.

And then

I notice the figure at the back.

The car slows to a stop,
the door opens,
and an umbrella pokes through,
a loud pattern of clashing colors.
It's Mala Nanda.

My blood runs cold.
I imagine the shadow that
her simple clothes
and humble ways
will cast against everything I'd said about
"my aunt."

She is still grappling with the umbrella,
half-hidden behind its large canopy,
when I sprint to the car,
not caring that I am getting drenched
in the drizzle that is now a shower,
and practically push her back in.

I didn't want you to get wet,
I offer as way of explanation
as I fall on top of her
into the safe confines
of the car.
Door firmly shut,
I exhale.

That had been way too close.

LIKE THE MOON

The following day

the whole classroom is abuzz.
A-what-an-amazing-party-buzz.

Nethmi can't stop showing off her new earrings.
The ones from yours truly.
Tiny blue sapphire studs, which I think are worth
quite a bit of money.
Nethmi wouldn't love them
as much if not.

Charity case

The earrings were a present from Sasha.
More like a donation.
They were so pretty I wanted them for myself.
But it's not like I could tell her,
Hey, so can I keep these and
can you give me something else
to give Nethmi?
All I did was thank her profusely.

Sasha said she didn't much care for them
and that if her parents asked

she could simply say
she lost them.
Given the chance
she might have even
thrown them away.
She does that with things
she has no use for anymore.

But now she has a better reason
to get rid of them.

Me!

My place

Whenever Madam sees me setting their table for dinner
she invites me to join them.

At first, it's rather awkward,
all that distance across the table,
waiting for someone to pass you food,
chewing softly.

Mala Nanda glares at me
as she refills the dishes.
I know what those silent stares mean.
You need to know your place.

A maid never sits
at the same level as their employers,

and always eats last,
usually whatever's left over.
What I'm doing is unheard of.
For a maid.

I don't tell her that my plans involve
being more than a maid
to the Madams and Sirs and Sashas
of this world.
I don't want to work for them.
I want to *be* them.

And somehow, I don't think
that's going to happen
by staying
in my place.

The villain

Apart from helping her clean up after dinner
and sleeping with her at night
I don't have time to hang out with Mala Nanda
as much as I'd like to.
But today I join her.

She is watching a Sinhala-dubbed Indian teledrama
like she does every night.
It's on its 621st episode
and doesn't show signs of ending anytime soon.
It's boring
but comforting.

I poke fun at her obvious delight
when the villainous mother-in-law in the show
finds new ways of torturing
her new daughter-in-law.
Mala Nanda defends the villain.
Young women should know to keep their head down
and listen to the older person in the relationship,
she argues.
If any woman, young or old, treats me like that
I'll give her a good earful,
I argue back.

As much as I hate to admit it,
the innocent daughter-in-law
reminds me of Siripala.
How he tries to make an effort.
How I never give him a chance.

Does that make me
the villainous mother-in-law?
Am I wrong to treat him the way I do?
It makes me feel a bit
guilty.

The last thing I see before sleep takes over that night
is an image of myself and Amma,
smiling at each other.
Which is what I dream about
most nights.

But tonight,
Siripala is there too,
smiling along with us.

First term tests

are next week.

It's hard to imagine it's been
less than three months
since I moved to the city.
It feels both longer (when I think of home)
and shorter (when I remember where I am)
at the same time.

In my old school I was always the first
every term,
every year.
I wonder where I'll rank in this class.

Sometimes I wish I was friends with the
other scholarship kids.
Their notes are complete
and they never miss a word the teacher says
because they're not busy whispering
or eating in secret
like us.

My usually neat books are now filled
with doodles in the margins—

names of new singers, bands, movies, gadgets—
things I need to learn
that aren't in any textbook.

The time I spend revising lessons every evening
has been taken over by Sasha and
I barely manage to fit in my homework
between my chores.

I have a feeling
I won't be first
this time.

Unplaced

is what I'll end up being
but I don't know that yet.

If I did,
maybe I would have tried harder
to be a better student
rather than trying
to be a better liar.

A good example

While my stomach forms nervous knots
as the exams draw closer,
my friends show no such signs

of discomfort.
I soon realize why.

Nethmi, Sulo, and I
are sitting under the madatiya tree.
The period before had not gone great.
The teacher had noticed me staring out the window
and had made me stand for the rest of the lesson
as punishment.

This has never happened to me before.
I am so used to being
the good example.
Look at how well Kavi is doing,
even with everything else going on in her life.
You must all strive to be like her,
Nayana teacher had once told the entire classroom.
A far cry from what my teachers
in this school
say about me.

Nethmi and Sulo are singing.
They don't notice my sadness.
Their biggest problem seems to be
figuring out the correct song lyrics.

I clear my throat.
Are you two ready for the exams?

Sulo stops singing.
Not really.

I'm okay with most of the subjects
except for math and Sinhala.
Amma said she wouldn't let me be in the choir this year
if my marks don't improve.

Nethmi groans.
I always score the lowest in math.
And science.
Thaththa will be so mad if I get below fifty again.

They go back to their singing.

Assumptions

I wonder what Nethmi's father would do
if she scored badly.
Not take her out for ice cream?
Make her watch less television?
Or maybe she'll have to make her bed
by herself for once.
(She has her own version of a Mala Nanda
to do it for her every day.)

My unvoiced questions
are soon answered by her.
Last time I scored badly,
he didn't talk to me for a month.
And he made Ammi pack away all my novels.

What?

How can you become a doctor
with measly marks like this?
You're such a disgrace!
She laughs as she mimics him,
but the laughter feels forced
and quickly changes to a frown,
and I watch as she moodily pulls
at a clump of grass.

My cheeks warm up
when I think of the assumptions
I made about her.

But that doesn't stop me
from taking the chance
to show off something
that I'm good at.
For a change.

Big mistake

I always score highest for those subjects, I say
trying to keep the smugness out of my voice.
I score well in all subjects really.
When I put in the work, that is.
They both stop singing at the same time.
They exchange a look.
A look I don't understand.

Cornered

Nethmi does it first.
Her eyes get smaller and beadier,
like the eyes of the kabaragoyas who emerge from roadside drains
and survey their surroundings before
sliding back in again.

Sulo looks confused for a second
and then her eyes grow rounder.
She avoids looking at me.
It's obvious she understands whatever it is.

It's as if they both know something
I don't.

Kaviiiiiii . . .
Nethmi drags the *i* in my name in a syrupy sweet tone.
Since we sit next to each other anyway,
you can help us,
can't you?

Reality check

I am so lost in thought
that I don't notice how quiet Ranjith is
when he picks me up.
How his eyes dart around,
how he drives faster than usual,
how he doesn't ask me how my day went.

I am so relieved that I don't have to relive it
that I stay silent too.

Nothing penetrates my daze,
not even the sirens of the ambulances
or the extra policemen and soldiers on the roads.
It's only when Mala Nanda rushes out
to embrace me as I get down from the vehicle
that I know something is wrong.
She is weeping.
I hear the blare of the news from inside the house.
All the TVs are turned on to
one channel.

My heart stops for a moment.
A bomb? I ask,
although I already know the answer.
Most news is bad news
when your country is at war
with itself.

She confirms my fears with a nod.
Where? I want to know.
Outside the main bus station in Colombo.

A breath of relief escapes me.
My village is safe.
Which means my family is safe.
Caring comes at such a cost
that it has a hierarchy.

Mala Nanda's shoulders shake with sobs.

The dead are mostly women and children.
Children like you, Kavi!
They were on their way home after school.

An LTTE suicide bomber had set off a bomb
in a bus full of civilians.
It's happened before.
We get reminded of the possibility of it daily
with each stop at a checkpoint,
with each reveal of the contents in our bags,
and each time our bodies are frisked
before we enter a place of importance.
But it doesn't get easier.

I stroke Mala Nanda's back,
feel her sobs subside as we watch
the footage of the carnage together.
Blood,
body parts,
loved ones wailing over
corpses covered in white sheets.

My mind flashes to
my bus ride with Siripala.
This could have been us.

Avurudu

Mala Nanda is feeding me dinner.
We are still watching the news

when the sad, serious voices are suddenly replaced
with a happy commercial jingle.
Advertisements for upcoming Avurudu sales.

Avurudu falls during the month of April.
It's what we call the Sinhala New Year,
which is also the same day as the Tamil New Year.

Sinhala—us.
Tamil—them.
I find it strange that we share such an auspicious day
with the ones we are fighting against.
If there was something as inauspicious as possible,
a war would be it.

Maybe it was decided
before someone drew the line that
divided us.

I ask Mala Nanda
what her plans for the April holidays are.
She smiles ruefully.
Same same, she says.

While holidays mean going home for me,
Mala Nanda doesn't have a home to go to.
Although Madam and Sir look after her so well,
Mala Nanda's "home" is still
this room.

Do you want to spend Avurudu with us?
I ask her.

I can visit, yes,
but not for the entire month.
They need me here, no?

I frown.
It's as if she can read my mind
because the next thing she says is,

Home for me means
peace of mind.
Without it,
anywhere you live
can be torture.
And with it,
even the prison cell
can be freedom.
This is my home,
my peace of mind.

I know what she means.

Pirith

That night I look for Mala Nanda's
well-used cassette tape of pirith.

I slot it in the player and as the
hypnotic chants fill my ears,
my thoughts fill with images of home.
Of our beautiful shrine,

of the times I'd sat in front of it,
listening to pirith like I'm doing now,
looking for a way to quieten my fears.

The time away has made me almost forget
how unhappy I was at home.
Although I wouldn't go as far as
to call it torture,
I sure am glad I don't have all that
to deal with over here.

Walls closing in

I replay what Nethmi and Sulo asked of me.
How they said that they wished they had my brains;
how if they did, then they would have helped me too;
how best friends have to help each other.

They have never asked anything of me before
(which is good because I don't have much to give)
and this is something I can easily do
for once.

But even thinking about it
makes my skin crawl
and my breath quicken.

It's like I'm seeing
the four walls of my prison
for the first time.

How do I get myself out of this one?

Take one

Me: *I haven't studied either.*
Sulo: *That's what you said for the monthly tests,
and you still scored in the nineties.*

Take two

Me: *There's no point copying from me,
because I'll probably get most of it wrong.*
Nethmi: *It'll still be less than what I would get wrong
without your help.*

Take three

Me: *What if we get caught?*
Sulo: *We won't. We'll teach you how to do it properly.*
Me: *You've done this before?*
No response.

Final blow

Nethmi: *I thought you were our friend, Kavi.
But you still haven't even invited us over to your
so-called amazing house.*

And now you're making such a fuss.
You can just tell us if you don't want to
hang out with us anymore.

Wait a minute.
So-called?

The big deal

Sasha is playing her Game Boy furiously,
not even giving me a turn.
I don't care.
I have bigger problems.

I think they know something, Podi Madam!
I still can't make myself call her by her name.
Doesn't "so-called" mean that you think
the other person is lying?
How do they know I'm lying?
And . . . and . . . they want me to cheat!
The words don't come out fast enough.

Sasha doesn't look up.
Before I can stop myself,
irritation forms itself into a loud
Tsk.

She pauses her game.

What's the big deal?

Just do it.
The teachers never notice.

I can hardly believe my ears.
When I speak my voice is so soft
that Sasha makes me repeat myself.
You cheat too?
It can't be.

She shrugs.
Sometimes.

But why?

Because it makes Amma and Thaththa happy.
They're very rarely happy,
in case you haven't noticed.
And when they're happy
they buy me whatever I ask for.
She is grinning while she says this,
as if it's a perfectly normal thing to do.

Just like Nethmi and Sulo.

But they buy you whatever you ask for anyway!
Why do you have to cheat and lie?
My voice is more than a whisper now.
I'm shouting but all I can hear
is a ringing in my ears.

Sasha is looking at me funny,
her smile gone.
And who are you
to tell me *what I should*
or shouldn't do?

Her words punch my stomach.
I imagine Mala Nanda
standing on my shoulder like the good angel,
reminding me of "my place."

But Sasha isn't done.
You have been lying to your friends
every
single
day,
and you were fine with
me helping you
do that.
But now suddenly
you're a Miss Goody Two-Shoes?
Well, news flash,
you're not!

With that, she goes into her room
and slams the door shut,
and I scurry back downstairs
to where I belong.

A true friend

Okay, I'll do it.
Tell me how?

Here we are,
the three of us,
heads bent together,
conspiring.
I don't like what we are conspiring about
but I'm glad I'm still
a part of something.

Sasha was right.
There isn't a huge difference
between lying and cheating.
They are practically the same thing.

Anyway, once I've done this
Nethmi and Sulo will know that
I'm a true friend,
willing to do anything for them.
And nothing will
change their minds.

Not even
the truth.

Poya Day

I pluck flowers from the garden,
arranging them in a basket
and sprinkling water on top
to help them stay fresh.

It's a Full Moon Poya Day, a national holiday,
and Mala Nanda is taking me to the temple.
It's one of the few times we are unaccompanied
and I look forward to it.

At the temple,
the stacks of pahan with their flickering flames
and the orange tips of incense sticks
frame the silhouettes of people walking about.

I love how we seem to blend in for once.
We all wear white,
our feet bare, our faces hopeful.
The prayers we utter in whispers
sound like everyone else's,
and we take turns at the taps to fill our pots with water
with which to bathe the bo tree,
just like everyone else.

Nobody cares about
who I am,
where I come from,
what my parents do for a living,
or how many Barbie dolls I own.

The eyes of the Buddha watch me
as I mindfully place
flower by flower
at his altar.
Does he know
that I have not been good lately?

Haven't you ever had to do things
you were uncomfortable with?
I ask him silently.

Everything I did made me uncomfortable,
I can almost hear him reply.
But it was for the greater good.

I'm satisfied with this response.
What I'm doing is for the greater good too!
I'm not only helping myself
but also my friends.

Being uncomfortable
is just an
unfortunate side effect.

Perspective

I look up at the sky
on our walk back to the house.
The clouds have cleared

and the moon beams down at us,
round,
white,
bright.

Mala Nanda stops walking
and follows my gaze upward.

Kavi, isn't it amazing how we see the moon differently
depending on which day of the month it is,
but the moon itself never changes?
The only thing that changes is
how much of it we see.

Huh.
She's right.
Why had that
never occurred to me before?

D-Day

The clock on the wall watches over us
like some all-seeing ruler.

The loud *tick tick*
is only interrupted by the sound of
pens scratching paper furiously
and the *creak creak*
of chairs being rocked on two legs
by their nervous inhabitants.

I'm not nervous.
It's the Sinhala exam
and I have finished answering all the questions
with forty-five minutes to spare.
At least I wasn't nervous before now.

Although our desks aren't touching anymore,
I see Sulo
stretch and straighten in front of me
as she waits.
The back of my head is warm.
It must be Nethmi's eyes burning a hole there
from behind.

The weather is muggy and now it's stifling.
The fan above turns at a lazy pace,
its purpose unfulfilled.
I loosen the knot of my tie.

Nethmi lets out a theatrical yawn.
The signal.

I wipe the dripping sweat pooled at my collar.
Then I slowly gather my answer sheets,
staple them securely,
and hold them firmly together in one hand.

The teacher at the front of the hall
is busy marking a set of papers
and a quick glance tells me
that the teacher behind isn't looking either.

I rock my chair back as far as I can
and move my arm downward and backward
still clutching the papers.
A baton waiting to be passed,
but this race is going in reverse
and I can't see my teammate.
Will I make it in time?

A tug and I let go
and almost collapse on my table in relief.

Just one more round to go.

Squirrels

I'm not sure when everything got messed up
but it did.
Badly.

It may have been when Nethmi
drops the papers on the ground as planned
but in typical Nethmi fashion,
draws too much attention picking them up.
I kneel to help and the teacher's voice
cuts through the quiet
like a megaphone in my ear.
Kavi, SIT DOWN NOW.
I jump in fright
and almost forget
to take my papers back

or

it might have been
when Sulo coughs her signal cough
before I'm ready.
The teacher is looking,
I'm sure of it.
Sulo coughs again.
And again.
What is wrong with her?

Someone announces,
Fifteen minutes more!
Oh, maybe that's why.

Everyone is looking at their papers again.
One final check before handing them in.
Sulo looks back,
her eyes pleading.
I don't have time to think.
The teachers are starting to pace again
and I can't leave Sulo hanging.

Just as I stretch out my arm toward her
and she reaches to take the papers from me,
mouthing the word *thanks*, she

freezes

and whips back around so quickly
it reminds me of squirrels playing happily

when you watch them from a distance,
but scurrying away frantically the minute
you take a step closer.

That's when I know that there's someone
who has been watching from a distance
and has taken a step closer.

Fangs

The perfume: strong.
The sari: blue.
The blood-red lips: curled in a snarl.
It's Ms. Pointy-Teeth Principal.

You three, she says in an icy voice,
pointing at Nethmi, Sulo, and me.
*I'll see you in my office
tomorrow after school.*

I think I'm starting to shiver
because my teeth are making sounds.
I will them to stop
but it only gets worse.

With your parents,
she adds,
before swishing away.

With your parents

An entire hall full of children
staring at us
and all I can think of
are those parting words.

Null and void

It takes a while for me to realize that
the dry, parched sensation in my throat
is not thirst but fear.

I stare at my two friends
looking for consolation or comfort
but all they do is look back at me
with such horror
(Sulo more than Nethmi
who is just biting her nails furiously)
that I know we are done for.

The teacher grabs our papers,
her mouth a straight, unrelenting line,
as if she can't bear to talk to us.
She takes out her red pen and, as we watch,
places a huge cross on each of them.

Null and void.

I have failed
my first big exam
at my new school.

That's when it comes crashing down on me.
I have been spending all my time
since I came here
preparing for the
wrong
test.

Crumbling

Ranjith, Mala Nanda, and I
are sitting on the porch steps
sharing a bag of roasted peanuts.
They're too busy having an animated conversation
about the country's state to notice that
I'm not eating.

I hold my share in my palm,
rolling each nut between my fingers
until the peel crumbles away,
feathery soft like butterfly wings.
I don't bother to separate the nuts
from amongst the ruins of
what was once their cocoon.
Their cover.

But I should.

I clear my throat.
Mala Nanda,
can I talk to you inside?

The next day

when I enter the examination hall
I don't feel welcome or accepted
or any of the things that I had
grown accustomed to.
It's like first day all over again
but with the hope replaced with
hopelessness.
The kids avoid my eyes
(maybe I'm avoiding theirs),
and the teachers look at me with such scorn
that I can't bear it.

During the interval,
between the day's exams,
we meet under the madatiya tree,
Nethmi, Sulo, and me.
We are quiet,
lifeless almost.
At least that's how I feel.
Like a deflated balloon.

Neither of them had called me yesterday
like I hoped they would.
I had thought they would have a backup plan

and that they would share it with me.

But as we eat in silence,
there is no planning
or conspiring.
They ask me if my parents are coming.
The food lodges in my throat.
They can't make it in time.
My aunt is coming,
I reply.

When I had told her last night,
Mala Nanda said that
everything would be all right.
But she doesn't know everything.
She only knows the parts I
chose to tell her.

Like the moon,
what others see
when they look at me
depends on
when they are looking.

A total eclipse

As far as backup plans go,
mine isn't so bad.
Mala Nanda is in her best cotton sari,
the pleats ironed to perfection.
So far,
so good.

Sure, the other parents are in
covered shoes with heels
while Mala Nanda's strappy sandals
are peeling in places.
And there is a distinct difference
between the strong perfume they wear
and the baby cologne she loves.

But she sits upright with an air of dignity,
and where there is distance between
the other parents and their daughters,
Mala Nanda's hand stays on my arm
reminding me that I am not alone.

She remains quiet while everyone takes their turn
speaking with the principal.
There are
explanations,
apologies,
excuses,
and even mentions of donations,
as if that is somehow relevant.

All the while, Nethmi and Sulo
keep glancing at Mala Nanda
and at each other.
Do they notice the differences
as much as I do?

This worries me so much
that I don't hear the question,

but I hear
the answer.

Nethmi stands up and looks at Sulo,
who looks away.
Neither of them look at me.
It was Kavi's idea, Madam Principal.
She said she did it all the time
back home.

I know then what they are doing.
Unbelievable.
I thought we were friends.

Nethmi's mother clears her throat.
I have told Nethmi that she should be careful
of the company she keeps.
But what can you expect
of this class of people?

Mala Nanda's tender hold on my arm
becomes a grip,
her fingers pressing into my flesh.

What do you mean?
asks the principal.

Nethmi's mom covers her mouth
as if she doesn't want to respond.
I wish she had kept it covered
because what she says next
makes my knees go weak.

The maid class, I mean.
She is looking right at Mala Nanda.

Defenseless

My jaw drops right at the same time
Mala Nanda gasps.
Her cheeks have lost their color,
her hand lets go of me,
and she crumples in her chair.

My blood begins to boil.
I am angry.
Angry with my friends,
angry with this school,
angry with my mother,
and my father,
and Siripala.

Most of all I am angry
with myself.

Usually when I'm angry
I shut down,
back off,
disappear.

Not today.

Mala Nanda didn't do anything wrong.

She came in unarmed
to fight for me,
and I won't let her
get hurt.

War cry

Now that I don't have anything to hide,
I let all my pretenses drop.
No more well-mannered,
eager-to-please,
pretend-rich girl.

I summon all my village-girl strength,
achieved through years of
sweat and tears,
and turn to Nethmi's parents.

Nethmi is the one who begged me
to share my answers . . . to cheat!
All because she didn't want to get punished
by you, her parents!
And now, she would rather put
the blame on me
than tell the truth!
Where's the class in that?
I always wished we had money,
but I'd rather be poor
than be so . . .
so . . .

My brain struggles to find a word
to communicate how
horrible I think they are,
so I do what Amma would have done.
I glare at Nethmi and . . .
Thoo!
I spit at her.
The ultimate denouncement.

I barely hear the scrape of the chair
as the principal stands up,
her finger pointing at the door,
her chin trembling.
But I'm not done yet.

Oh, and we might be maid-class,
but we wouldn't work for people like you
even if you paid us in gold!

I storm off,
tears streaming down my face,
not caring about the stunned looks
on everyone else's.
I never want to set foot
in this awful place
ever again.

CONFRONTATIONS
AND
CONFESSIONS

Shattered

I cry
till my nose is blocked,
till my mouth runs dry,
till my tears are used up.

But the shame inside me refuses to lessen.

Shame that I made the wrong choices,
shame that I ruined this opportunity,
shame that I wanted more,
instead of being happy
with all that
I already had.

I had called Nethmi a liar,
but I wasn't any better than her.
All I had done
was lie.
The more I think about it,
the worse I feel.

Mala Nanda shakes me gently every few hours,
reminding me to eat,
wash up,

step out of the room.
But I don't want to move.

If I don't get out of this bed,
if I don't open my eyes,
I can pretend I'm still dreaming.

That none of this happened.
That my world hasn't fallen apart

again.

Maid-class

A lot had happened since my departure
from the principal's office that day.

It was Nethmi's mother
who had recognized Mala Nanda.
She and Sasha's dad had been friends a long time ago
and she had remembered Mala Nanda
from her visits to this house as a teenager.
It didn't take long for her to
connect the dots
and make those dots known
to everyone present.
About who I really was
and how my cheating
had gone beyond
just the exam.

Which means
Nethmi knows,
Sulo knows,
the principal knows,
Mala Nanda knows.

None of them say a word to me about it.
Although that's because
three of those four people
don't want anything to do
with a cheating,
maid-class,
village girl.

Moonbeams

The mattress sags and creaks
as Mala Nanda settles in to sleep
next to me.

It's pitch-dark
except for a sliver of light
from where she hasn't drawn the
curtain entirely closed.
The moonbeams touch me,
and I play with the shadows.
I wonder if they are touching
Amma tonight too.
If she is alone
or with Siripala.

And then I remember
the baby inside her.
Even if she is alone,
she will never be
lonely.

I wish I was still a baby too,
cradled by Amma
every single second of the day.
And suddenly there's nothing
I want more
than to be with her.

I turn to Mala Nanda and say,
I want to go home,
my words muffled by the pillow.
Mala Nanda clutches my hand,
her eyes shiny in the faint light.
Okay.

Numb

It's a school day
but I'm busy packing.

They call it suspension—
two weeks before the end of the term.
I call it an extra-long break.
Well, not really a break
since I'm not coming back.

Holding it together

The zipper on my bag has its work cut out,
trying to hold everything inside.

The meager collection
I had come with
is just a fraction of
what I am leaving with.
I finger the pretty clothes and shoes
and toys and books.
Everything Sasha has given me.

I haven't spoken to her since that awful day,
the one where she said all those horrible things.

But I have to say goodbye.

Careless vs. caring

The door to Sasha's bedroom is closed.
I knock.
No answer.
I take a deep breath
and push the door open.

Sasha notices me
and removes her earphones.
We both listen to the tinny sounds
coming from them.

I sit down next to her.
She still doesn't speak
and then we both speak
together.

Podi Madam, I never should have done what I did . . .
Kavi, Amma told me what happened at school . . .

We both pause,
look at each other.

Sasha continues,
twirling her finger around the wires of her earphones.
Kavi, it's all my fault.
I should have warned you about
kids in the city.
They can be careless.

Like me, she adds,
more to the dolls watching us
than to me,
but I hear her.
I didn't expect that.
Sasha never admits her faults.
But that's what friends do,
a voice in my head whispers,
and it's as if a weight is lifted.

Nethmi and Sulo, they were careless, I tell her.
Friends who only want you for something
and don't stand by you,

they're useless.

The memory festers inside me like a wound.
But as Mala Nanda says,
I'm lucky to have figured it out now
rather than later.

I should never have done any of it.
I am a bad girl.
Now I will have to pay for my sins,
I say quietly.

The only reason

Sasha is next to me in two strides
hugging me,
her hair smelling of her expensive shampoo.
Oh, Kavi, you are so dramatic!
You're not bad.
You just did *something bad.*
I did too.
I should have known better than to egg you on.
At least that's what Amma and Thaththa told me.
They gave me an earful last night!
She says this with glee,
as if being scolded by your parents is something
to be happy about.

Podi Madam,
why do you like to get into trouble with your parents?

I hate it when my amma is angry with me.
(Even though I can be plenty angry with Amma.
But that is for a good reason,
so it doesn't count.)

Kavi, what rock do you live under?
Haven't you heard them fighting?
The only reason they're together is because of me.
Disciplining me is one of the few times
they take each other's side.
Sasha's tone is light,
but I know she's struggling
to share this with me.

I am both shocked and confused.
Shocked because I thought rich people
don't have a reason to be unhappy,
and confused because,
So . . . you get into trouble
just to see them together?

Yeah, I guess. She shrugs,
walking to the TV lounge,
and as I follow her
I realize that she too
is mourning a loss.

She turns on the TV and it's *Dawson's Creek.*
Okay, so since I'm trying to be a better friend,
I should warn you that this is probably

too grown-up for you,
Sasha tells me,
covering my eyes with her hand.
I don't have the heart to tell her that,
since this would be my first and last time watching it,
it won't matter.
We only have four TV channels in the village,
and none of them show *Dawson's Creek.*

I push her fingers away.
Oh, please,
I know what they do behind the blurry squares!

Goodbyes

It's my last day in this house
that I had thought would be my home.
But if I'm not going back to school,
I have no reason to stay.

Well, I try to find one.
I ask Mala Nanda if I can be a maid like her
and she glares at me and tells me to
stop talking nonsense.
(There's also the little problem
of it being illegal to not go to school.)
I'm sure you'll change your mind
once you go home,
she says.

Yes, because I'll be the third wheel in
Amma's new happy family,
I mutter under my breath.
As much as I don't want to come back here,
I also worry about being back home.

Mala Nanda sighs.
You know that's all in your head.
She starts the lecture I know by heart now.
Your amma loves you.
She may not be the best at showing it,
but she does everything with your future in mind.
Blah, blah, blah.

To which I say,
Well, then how come she hasn't
told me that herself?
That shuts her up.

My heart fills with an unexplainable sadness
as I walk through all the rooms in the house.
Everything is still,
everyone is asleep.

I run my fingers on
the lifeless gray screen of the television,
the icy cool marble kitchen counters,
and the vehicles (all three of them).
I stand outside Madam and Sir's room
(Sasha says that they sleep in the same room
to pretend to her that they are together)

and fervently hope they fall in love with each other again.
Finally, I place a wrapped gift outside Sasha's room.
It's a copy of *Dil to Pagal Hai*,
the Hindi movie we all watched together at the cinema.
She fell asleep watching it that time,
but I know it'll remind her of me this time.

The three of them refused to say goodbye to me.
They don't believe I'm not coming back,
doing their best to convince me that I should.

And as I board the bus back home,
I wish they had succeeded.

Window seat

Siripala is taking me home.

Ever seen a lorry full of coconuts
packed to the brim
threatening to spill over?
That's how crowded this bus is.
I'm grateful for my coveted window seat
which gives me room to
breathe.

Siripala fought someone for it.
He might not be an army officer
fighting for his motherland,
but the way he

scrambled,
jostled,
and heaved himself onto that seat
was valiant.
Especially since
he gave it up seconds later
for me.
He is standing.
Going on his third hour now.
I almost feel sorry for him.

We stop midway for a tea break.
The bus we get back into
is much emptier.
Our village is remote.
Not many leave it,
and if they do,
they often don't
return.

A rare chat

This time Siripala sits next to me.
The traffic and fumes give way
to fields and trees.

Siripala strikes up a conversation.
Maybe it's the overdose of sugar in the tea we drank,
or the fact that we have three more hours together
ahead of us.

He seems changed—
more talkative and cheerful.
Either way,
I welcome the distraction.
Maybe I've changed too.

*Your mother is so big now
she can't do half of what she used to*, he says
between mouthfuls of the tea bun
we are sharing.
But instead of saying this accusatorily
like most men in the village would,
Siripala sounds proud.

*So who looks after the farm then?
And the animals?*
I'm too curious to ignore him.

I do.

His words stick with me.
They make me wonder
if there's more to Siripala
than what
I have chosen to see.

Lulled by these thoughts
and the rhythmic
start-stop
start-stop
jerkiness of our ride,

I fall into what seems like
the first proper sleep I've had
in days.

The voice inside

Amma doesn't greet us at the bus stand,
but is waiting for us at home instead.
She looks so beautiful
and smells so good
that I can't help but embrace her shyly.

Her enormous stomach gets in the way,
a reminder that very soon
I'll be ousted forever.
But as she bends to
kiss the top of my head like she used to,
I hear the voice inside my head,
the one that's gotten very noisy lately.
The one that tells me that
maybe I'm wrong about her.
The one I hope
is right.

Armor

I shed my "Colombo" layers eagerly,
switching my funky T-shirts and leggings
for the more comfortable flowery dresses,

speaking loudly without having to use hushed tones,
and running everywhere barefoot
without being afraid of
knocking over any valuables.

Then I remember the "village" layers
I shed before I left.
The ones that are here
still waiting for me.
The ones with lots of armor
to protect me from all the hurt I felt.

Do I need to
put them on
again?

Connection

It's Poya again.
The moon is out in all its glory.
Unconcealed.

Amma oils my hair,
her hands working their magic.
She doesn't make a move to leave.
She must be tired from our walk
around the temple earlier today.
The jasmine blooms dot the darkness,
bright white on inky black,
their scent stronger than ever.

I relax under Amma's touch,
feel emboldened by her closeness.
I lean back,
back,
back
till my head rests
on her chest.
Thud,
thud,
thud.
Her heartbeat is faster than mine,
and then,
a kick so fierce I yelp.

That's your baby sister, Kavi.
Your nangi.
Amma guides my hand over her bump.
A wriggle,
another kick,
a perfect moment.

I mentally pack
all my armor away.

A new ritual

Every morning,
Siripala places Amma's cup of tea beside her
before he leaves for work.
He doesn't wake her up.

A far cry from the sleeping lump
he used to be.

Now that I think about it,
maybe he was just
a tired man
sleeping in.
And maybe Amma
not minding
was
love.

About what happened

If Amma knows,
she hasn't asked me.
I'm thankful.
Because I'm not ready
to tell her.

Not yet

Not while my old doubts
still simmer beneath this
fragile new state of things.
This temporary ceasefire.

I watch Amma sleep.
Her body is still but for her belly,

which moves and stretches.
A life of its own.

Amma's eyelids flit and flutter.
I wonder if she's thinking of the baby.
I wonder if everything will get worse again,
when it's finally,
finally
getting better.

Concern

Siripala and I are eating dinner on our porch,
trying not to make too much noise.
Amma has always been a light sleeper,
and she struggles even more now.

Our dinner is delicious.
The neighboring aunties bring
an endless supply of freshly cooked curries,
local staples for mothers-to-be.
Jackfruit that falls apart when you touch it,
sticky breadfruit coated in coconut milk,
chunks of sharkfish in spicy gravy.
I have saved some of the curry we got
for Siripala.
I serve this to him silently.

I wipe my plate clean with my fingers
and lick them,

savoring every last bit,
something I only do
at home.

I notice Siripala staring at me,
the curry on his hands congealing
as he waits for me to finish.
Embarrassed, I stop
and question him with my eyes.

Kavi,
I hope you'll go back to your new school
when the holidays are done.

My cheeks heat up.
Does he know?

Why, you want to get rid of me again?
I'm annoyed and the words spill out,
loud and harsh.

You need to believe me when I say
that is not the case.
His voice is calm,
his words deliberate.

I don't.
But I want to.
I try again.
Why then?

Convincing

Kavi, you're such a clever child.
You must get it from your mother.
She's so smart.
She can do almost anything,
but she can't read or write.
It's one of her biggest regrets.

Your new school
is one of the best in the country,
and you get to go there for free!
You'll do things you regret.
But don't let this be
one of them.

Restless

It's nearly a week since I came home and
I'm already restless.
It wouldn't have been so bad if Sunil was here
but he's gone to his grandparents' in the next village.

I'm tempted to hop on a bus and go see him,
but Amma says no.
There's a war.
No going about unless
absolutely necessary.
The usual reason.

Sigh.
I can't wait for this stupid war
to be over.

Messengers

I'm busy scraping coconut,
my back to the door,
when Nayana teacher visits.

Kavi?
Someone calls me from outside.
Aaaahhh?
I reply, still scraping.
Watching the white shreds accumulate
to become a grated coconut mountain
makes me happy.

Can I come in?

That's when I recognize the voice.
I drop the coconut half I'm holding
and rush to worship and welcome her.
Nayana teacher asks me how Colombo is,
how my new school is.

It's . . .
I struggle to find the words
that aren't a lie
but aren't the truth.

Difficult,
I say.

Nayana teacher's eyes search for mine.
New beginnings always are.
You went from the village to the city.
I came from the city to the village.
I know what it's like.

I meet her eyes.
They tell me what her words don't.

New beginnings won't always be new.
Soon what's strange will be your norm,
and things won't be so
difficult.

I try to imagine what my life
would have been like
without her.
If she hadn't made it past the new,
if this life hadn't become her norm,
I wouldn't have had
my own new beginning.
I don't want everything
she's gone through
to have been
in vain.

I remember Siripala's words
from the day before.

It can't be a coincidence.

Maybe it's Thaththa again,
sending me his
messengers.

Emergency

Getting caught cheating
was the scariest day of my life.

But when Amma wakes up at midnight
screaming,
writhing,
yelling
in pain,
a fear engulfs me so totally
that soon my screams are one
with hers.

The neighbors rush in
and Siripala carries Amma out.
He stops and turns back.
Kavi, what are you waiting for?
Come.

Don't go

I squeeze Amma's hand
as the tuk-tuk we're in races to the hospital.
I taste the saltiness of the tears
I didn't know I was shedding,
and that scared, sad part of me
finally breaks through.
Please, Amma, don't leave me.
I know you don't love me like you used to,
but it's enough.
Please don't go,
please don't go,
I chant,
willing her not to die.

Amma's grip on my hand tightens.
Kavi, I must have done
lots of good in my past lives
to have you as my daughter,
and if I die,
I hope you will be born to me
in my next life
and the next.
That's how much I love you
and always will,
no matter what.
But—she winces—
I'm not dying.
I'm giving birth.

And then she is screaming again.

Rebirth

If that's what giving birth is like
I don't ever want to have kids.

My baby sister is tiny,
a warm, squirming bundle
sucking greedily at Amma's breast,
blissfully unaware of the struggle and pain
she had caused coming out
just hours earlier.

I am the first to see her,
even before Siripala.
I sit with Amma till she finishes feeding
and she hands my sister over to me.
She looks just like you,
Amma says,
looking straight at me.
Her eyes are so full of it.
So full of love.

At that moment I feel like
I have been born
too.

Job description: Mother

Becoming a mother again
seems to have reminded Amma
of her job description.

She has started to fuss over me
in a way she never did before
(I love it),
and she watches Nangi and me
with this dreamy look on her face.
I would never have described Amma
as dreamy before.
She never had time to dream.

She seems much more relaxed now too.
More than she did when Thaththa was alive.

I recently found
a faded picture of him
under her pillow.

I felt so guilty, Kavi,
to even think of being with someone else
after your father.
He was so good to us
but the war changed him,
she says
when she catches me looking at it.
He was so miserable
after he lost his leg.

Nothing could make him happy again.
And after he died,
I thought nothing would make
me happy again
either.

Her hand flits over Nangi
before settling on me.
But look at this.
Look at us.

This time
she doesn't hide her tears
and neither do I.

Second chances

Siripala is not so bad after all.
He washes the baby,
boiling the water,
dipping his elbow into it a dozen times
till it reaches just the right temperature.
When she cries,
he rocks her for hours,
singing off-key lullabies
that would scare monsters away
but work on cranky babies
like a charm.

If not for Nangi,
I would never see
this side of him.

It makes me
question,
reconsider,
reevaluate.

Maybe sometimes
we all need
a second chance.

A letter

When the postman brings me a letter,
I think it must be from Sunil,
replying to the postcard I had sent
ordering his swift return.
But it's from Sasha.
Her letter is in English
but I can read most of it easily now,
something I couldn't do last year.

Two parts of it stand out.

The first part is:
I finally watched that super-long Hindi film
you left for me

and guess what?
I loved it!
I even memorized the songs.
I can't wait till you come back to watch it with you!

And the second part is:
Sulo came here looking for you
with some butter cake she had made.
I gave her a bit of a hard time
(you know me, I couldn't help myself!).
She admitted that it had all been
that snitch Nethmi's idea.
I told her she better grow a spine
or she couldn't be your friend again,
and she actually looked sorry.
Sorry, and a bit scared of me. Haha!
Maybe she's worth forgiving after all?
Also, she makes a superb butter cake!

I read them over and over again,
savoring each word in my mouth.

Start to finish

I don't want anything left unsaid
between Amma and me
so I tell her all that happened.
What I did.
Start to finish.

I don't think I've ever seen her
listen so intently.
Her reactions are priceless,
changing from happy to sad
to shock to disbelief
in mere minutes.

The best part is when I tell her about
how I stood up for Mala Nanda.
She claps!

And when I say,
I think I want to go back after all,
she turns to my nangi and says,
You see how brave your akka is?
You're lucky you have such a
good example.

The good kind

It's my last day at home
before I head back to the city.

Back to Mala Nanda and Ranjith,
back to Sasha, Madam, and Sir,
back to school,
back to Sulo.
(Not Nethmi,
never Nethmi.)

This time when I leave
I will be sad,
not because I am not loved,
but because I'm loved
so much.

The good kind of sad.

Something like that

I'm at the tea shop buying milk toffees
when someone taps my shoulder.
I turn around and see my dearest friend.
Sunil, you're back!

I'm sure my smile reaches my ears just like his.
We walk over to the concrete bund
and I share my toffees with him.
You're just in time.
I thought I wouldn't get to see you before I go back!
I have so much to tell you!

He lifts his hand to stop me.
Wait, let me guess.
The city is amazing,
your school is huge,
you came first in every subject,
and you didn't make any friends because
there's no one better than me.

I almost choke on my laughter,
sending milk toffee crumbs flying into his face.

Yeah, something like that!

My new norm

The familiar melody of the bread van
reaches my ears
as I divide my hair into two
and start plaiting.

I take out the two black ribbons
that Amma gave me
and secure the end of each plait
in a neat bow.

I walk up to the tiny altar
and lay the flowers I've plucked,
one by one,
and say my prayers to Lord Buddha.
I don't promise to not break any Pansil,
but I do promise
I'll try.

And I have tried.
It's been two months
since I've been back.
I've told everyone the truth,

I've apologized,
I've worked hard.

I'm still not near being the first in class,
and Nethmi still shoots daggers at me.
But I don't mind.

I have a family who loves me:
two families if you count
my real family back home
and my new family over here.

I have friends who love me:
Sunil writes every week;
Sasha is teaching me swimming;
and Sulo laughs at all my jokes.

And best of all,
I'm even starting
to love
myself.

Mala Nanda walks in.
Hurry up, child!
Sasha and Ranjith are already in the car.
Go now
or you'll be late for school!
I grab my shoes and rush out
with an ease I hadn't felt
until recently.

Maybe my new beginning
has finally become
my new norm.

I know now

that I can leave
without letting go.

That I can have new things
without forgetting the old.

That I can make mistakes
but also make them right.

That even when my life
changes,
shifts,
transforms,
I can still be me.
The real me.

I am and will always be
Kavi.

The Sri Lankan Civil War

The Sri Lankan civil war spanned almost thirty years from 1983 to 2009. It was fought between the Sinhala-dominated Sri Lankan government forces and the Liberation Tigers of Tamil Eelam (LTTE), an insurgent group that wanted a sovereign, separate state in the northern and eastern provinces of the country.

Sri Lanka's history dates back almost 2,500 years—ours is a civilization rich in culture and tradition. The Sinhalese are believed to have originated from the Aryans in North India; and the Tamils, who are the country's largest minority, are believed to have originated from the Dravidians in South India. Both occupied varying levels of power in the various royal kingdoms that the country was divided into throughout history.

The island's prime location in the Indian Ocean meant Sri Lanka eventually became home to a number of other ethnically diverse groups of people, such as the Muslims (arriving through trade connections) and the Burghers (descendants of Dutch colonizers). The country also had a diverse religious landscape; the Sinhalese were mainly Buddhist, the Tamils were mainly Hindus, the Muslims followed Islam, and later, many groups converted to Christianity, introduced by colonial missionaries. Despite the differences between all these communities, they coexisted, for the most part, in harmony.

Many believe that the foundation for the civil war was laid long before the documented combat started: with colonization. Sri Lanka was colonized for more than four centuries, first by the Portuguese, then the Dutch, and finally, by the British. The latter's colonial policies succeeded in creating a rift between the Sinhalese and Tamils. For example, Sinhalese schools, especially in rural areas, weren't developed by the British and offered only a basic education, while most Tamils, who lived in the north, had access to well-funded English schools. This allowed the British to offer a disproportionately high number of coveted bureaucratic positions in the government as well as competitive higher education opportunities—for which fluency in English and academic excellence were a prerequisite—to Tamil nationals, which gave the Tamil community a significant advantage over their Sinhala-speaking counterparts.

Once Sri Lanka gained independence from the British in 1948, the ruling political elite put into action laws to give more opportunities to the Sinhalese as a method of correcting this imbalance. A key reform included making Sinhala the official language of the country. This made it harder for Tamils to secure jobs in the civil service, which now required fluency in Sinhala. Therefore, instead of correcting the imbalance as intended, the balance was tipped once again, this time in favor of the Sinhalese. The now-marginalized Tamil community felt disrespected and unwanted, which set in motion a series of protests to which the Sri Lankan state and the Sinhalese responded with violence.

The Sri Lankan government set up military points around the country to monitor the situation. The disharmony, mounting after months of attacks and counterattacks by both sides, reached a boiling point when the now-formed Tamil Tigers killed thirteen army soldiers in July 1983. In retaliation, the Sinhalese attacked Tamil civilians all over the country, killing them and looting their homes and businesses. It was a dark period in Sri Lanka's history, one that officially marked the beginning of the war, and is referred to as "Black July."

The decades that followed saw a lot of bloodshed, with thousands of lives lost on both sides. The Tamil Tigers were recognized as a terrorist organization, as they resorted to ruthless tactics such as forcefully deploying child soldiers and suicide bombers. In turn, many young Sinhalese men and women joined the tri-forces, proud to be fighting to protect their country, seeing it as a noble deed, like Sunil. But it wasn't the only reason—most of them were poor, like Kavi's father, and being in the army was an assurance of a steady income for their families, even after their death.

The worst of the fighting happened in the northeastern parts of the country, with guerrilla warfare tactics being used, including Claymore mine attacks like the one to which Kavi's father lost his leg. The rest of Sri Lanka wasn't completely safe either. Colombo, where the top officials of the government lived, was often the target of political assassinations and bomb attacks on civilians. For example, the bomb blast that Kavi and Mala Nanda watch on the news is loosely based on an actual attack by the LTTE in Maradana, Colombo, where a minibus full of explosives was blown up by a suicide bomber, killing and injuring many civilians. The country's tourism industry, which is a livelihood for many and a major source of foreign income, also suffered as Sri Lanka was considered an unsafe destination for tourists. Reporting on the latter stages of the war, in particular, was censored, with the government preventing access to the conflict areas and many reporters and journalists risking their lives to tell the truth about alleged war crimes by the government forces.

The war finally came to an end in May 2009, when the Sri Lankan military defeated the Tamil Tigers. According to the Sri Lankan government, it is estimated that around one hundred thousand lives were lost owing to the war, although this figure is disputed as being an underestimation, with reports claiming that thousands of Tamils were killed during the final battle alone. Thousands of Tamil people were forced to flee the island that was their home, seeking asylum in other countries or becoming refugees in their own country—or they simply went missing.

However, the cost of any war goes beyond the numbers. How do you measure the value of a human life? How do you measure the grief of those hurt or left behind? How do you measure the trauma and fear that is passed down from generation to generation? And finally, when and how does a country heal? At the time of writing, it's been twelve years since the war ended. Neither side has claimed accountability for the human rights violations and war crimes committed, post-war reconciliation to restore unity among communities has been weak, and Sri Lankans are left with more questions than answers.

Acknowledgments

The desire to write my own novel would never have been born if I had not fallen in love with the writing of these amazing books by Sri Lankan writers that left a deep impression on me: *Five to Eight* by Indrasoma de Silva, *The Waiting Earth* by Punyakante Wijenaike, *July* by Karen Roberts, *Sam's Story* by Elmo Jayawardena, *What Lies Between Us* by Nayomi Munaweera, and *Wave* by Sonali Deraniyagala. It made me realize that stories authentic to our identity and history are as beautiful as they are necessary. It made me want to attempt to do the same.

Love and gratitude to my closely knit circle of writer friends from all over the world, first and foremost my mentor, David LaRochelle, for his constant guidance, wisdom, and gentle kindness. Then comes my critique groups, a vital component of my writing journey. My middle-grade writing critique group (or should I say support group?), the MG Waves, namely Jenny, Malia, Ranjeeta, Anushi, Karyn, Melissa, Beth, Kathryn, Sarah, TC, Taylor, Peggy Sue, Gemma, Morgan, Anne, Susan, Amy, Catie, Dawn, Imogen, Rebecca, Sonya, Anna, and Maureen; my first-ever picture book critique group, comprising Jessica, Karyn, Cindy, and Brian; and my critique group of verse novelists, Ranjeeta, Dawn, Amy, and Christy. Sharing all my ups and downs in publishing (and life!) with you has been a joy and I cannot wait to meet you in person someday. I also loved being a part of the 2023 Debuts and MGin23 groups; the energy everyone puts towards boosting each other's book babies has been an incredible thing to witness.

Thank you to those initial reviewers of Kavi, the ones whose words were make-or-break: Reem Faruqi, Melissa Jenson, Karyn Curtis, Gemma Stringer, Anna Vosburgh, Beth Gawlik, Natasha Holmes, and Nicole Hewitt. I'm so glad they were all encouraging and constructive in their feedback. I appreciate the time taken by my young beta readers Lakshmi Calleri, Tara Dias, and Ada Reitz to read the book and respond to my questionnaire about it. To Lindsay Flanagan, who handled this manuscript with so much attention and for copy checking it before submission: I appreciate all of it.

Thank you to those who guided me on sensitively framing the conflict: Padma Venkatraman, Sheshadri Kottearachchi, Gehan Gunatilleke, Amalini deSayrah, and Nithyani Anandakugan—your expertise was invaluable. My gratitude to those who have always been an email or message away with advice about publishing: Nizrana Farook, Hallee Adelman, Saba Sulaiman, Reem Faruqi, and Catherine Bakewell among so many others. Special gratitude to local author Amanda Jayatissa, who guided me through the entire process of writing for the American market from Sri Lanka. I didn't think it was possible till she did it—so successfully—herself.

Sashini, Tracy, Prabashi, Zahara, Nimmi, Apsi, Nilmini, and Nishanthi, and all my other friends and relatives who always respond so enthusiastically to my publishing news—I'm so glad to have you in my life. Shout-out to everyone who supports me on social media, from Sri Lanka and beyond, who engage with my gazillion tweets, who always cheer me on.

To my wonderfully kind and talented editor, Mora Couch at Holiday House, for believing in Kavi and me so strongly from the start. Your excitement and vision for this book and what it can achieve gave me so much confidence and hope. With you as an advocate, I'm sure we'll be able to help Kavi soar! Thanks also to the amazing team at Holiday House: Miriam Miller, Sara DiSalvo, Michelle Montague, Bree Martinez, Kade Dishmon, Rebecca Godan, Nicole Gureli, Kerry Martin, Lisa Lee, Judy Varon, Julia Gallagher, and many others.

To Jacqui Lipton, agent extraordinaire, who I connected with instantly. Thank you for "getting" me—you always understand just what I and my stories need. For all the times you virtually held my hand or called me back from the ledge when bad news came and sent air hugs and lots of exclamation marks when the good news came: I'm so glad we are a team.

Words aren't enough to express what I want to say to my parents, Ajanthi and Vijitha de Silva. My mother wasn't a reader at all, but she always encouraged my love for reading, even knocking on neighbour's doors to see if they had any books her daughter could borrow, and my father would wait patiently at bookshops while I took hours to browse, although he never bought any for himself. Both of them never hesitated to deliver when I would ask for a book—or a bookshelf!—and would always listen to those early drafts of essays and stories so encouragingly. I owe them everything.

To my in-laws, especially Kshama and Alex Ponweera, for being the second set of parents I've been blessed with: thank you for being so supportive and proud of me, and for opening up your haven of a home whenever I needed to rest, write, or escape!

To my second set of hands and eyes at home, Lakshmi, who was there from the beginning of my writing journey, and who I hope will someday be able to read a translation of my book: I appreciate all you do for me and my family.

To my husband, Rajiv, for listening to every line I wrote, for reading them out loud countless times so I could hear what they sounded like, for copy checking, brainstorming, praising, and telling everyone I'm an author while I blush furiously. I wouldn't have written this book if not for you.

To my darling son, Dhevan, and my daughter, Rahya: nothing could make me happier than the fact that the two of you will have this book to read written by your mother. Kavi has a lot of what I would wish for you both. She is brave and courageous; she dares to find hope even when things seem hopeless; she is fiercely loyal; she loves generously and trusts easily yet understands the value of being true to herself. And like Kavi's Amma, I too want only life's best things for you, and will love you no matter what else may change. Thank you for being you.

Author's Note

I first wrote about Kavi in a short story when I was seventeen years old. My life was unlike Kavi's in that I was privileged enough not to grow up in poverty, or lose a loved one to the war, or have to live away from my family at a young age. I grew up in the city and attended a good school—one that I did not have to win a scholarship to attend.

Where Kavi and I are similar, though, is that we both grew up amidst a war. I am Sinhalese-Buddhist, and although I have tried to present events through as neutral a lens as possible, I am aware that I may have unconscious biases which make this difficult to achieve. Please know that it is not my intention to cause offense.

Between 1983 and 2009, Sri Lanka endured a brutal war. I was born in 1984, right when the war broke out. But in Colombo, where I lived, the war was something that happened on television, something we read in the newspapers (a heavily censored version; we had no internet!), and was the inevitable conversation topic we overheard among our parents and their friends at every social gathering.

Things began to feel serious when the city became the target of bomb attacks.

I still remember the ground vibrating in the aftermath of a loud boom while I sat in my grade 6 class. I ran to the windows with a friend to watch the rising spirals of smoke; afterward, I waited in line at the school office to call my mother, so I could make sure my parents were unharmed. Schools began to close for weeks at a time in light of increased security threats, and although I was bored at home, I still managed to talk to and meet up with my friends or attend extracurricular activities.

More than a decade later, in 2007, I was watching the Cricket World Cup final on TV with my father at night when there was a power outage and a barrage of frantic phone calls from our relatives. I ran to the balcony to witness an air raid between the Army and the LTTE—I thought it looked like a meteor shower.

What I'm trying to say is that despite all of this, I and those around me were fortunate to be able to live relatively normal lives—complete with the everyday struggles that come with growing up, war-ravaged country or not. Even for Kavi, many of her problems (just like many of my problems) could have easily been those of a child growing up in a country where peace prevailed: struggling to fit in and be accepted, needing love and security, finding one's identity, and trying to make sense of the world.

But, as an adult, I learned that growing up so immune to war, as we did, is not actually normal. It just felt normal at the time. This is what led me to dig in and explore the very idea of "normalcy" in this story.

With the advent of the internet and social media, many varied accounts of the war were exposed, especially from those who lived in the north and in border villages during the war. It is now apparent just how destructive it actually was, and how it led and still leads to many unhappy endings. This is possibly why, when I embarked on writing as a career, Kavi's story became my first novel.

I wanted to write a story of hope—one with a happy ending despite all the challenges.

I wrote this book in the latter part of 2020, while the entire world was going through yet another far-from-normal period: the COVID-19 pandemic. But again, even when life as we knew it was falling apart, it also went on. I, for one, turned to writing. And you holding this book in your hand, reading it, means something really good came out of a dark period; something I'm very proud of.

It goes to show that human beings have the ability to adapt and overcome anything. To create our own sense of "normal."

I hope you remember that.

And like Kavi, should you get lost, I hope you find the strength inside you to find your way back. To know that your experience, even if different, is still valid; is still "normal."

THUSHANTHI PONWEERA

Glossary

Amma	Mother
Akka	Older sister
Ambulthiyal	A distinct preparation of fish that helps preserve it
Avurudu/ Puthandu	Sinhala & Tamil New Year festival
Baila	A form of music popular in Sri Lanka
Bo tree	Banyan tree that represents the tree under which Lord Buddha was enlightened
Ehela flowers	*Cassia fistula*, better known as Golden Showers
Kabaragoya	Asian water monitor
Karma	The force created by a person's past actions that some people believe causes good or bad things to happen to that person. In Buddhism it is believed this is carried on to the person's next life too.
Kiribath	Rice prepared with coconut milk
Kohomba tree	Neem tree

Loving-kindness	Buddhist practice of extending selfless/altruistic love toward all beings
Madatiya tree	*Adenanthera pavonina* or Red Bead Tree
Mallung	A Sri Lankan dish comprising lightly cooked, finely shredded leaves, shredded coconut, and other spices/condiments
Nanda	Aunt
Nangi	Younger sister
Padura	Mat woven out of coconut or palmyrah leaves
Pahan	Small clay lamps
Pansil	Five precepts in Buddhism
Parippu	Red lentils
Pirith	Buddhist chantings
Podi Madam	Small madam
Pota	The falling end of the sari
Poya	Full moon day that is religiously significant for Buddhists
Redda	Cloth that's wrapped tightly around the wearer's waist and extends to the wearer's ankles. Worn by women.

Sarong	Cloth that's wrapped loosely around the wearer's waist and extends to the wearer's ankles. Worn by men.
Thaththa	Father
Thunuruwan Saranai	Blessings of the Triple Gem
Triple Gem	The three jewels of Buddhism: Buddha (The Enlightened One), Dhamma (the teaching of the Buddha), Sangha (the monastic community of Buddhist disciples)
Tuk-tuk	Three-wheeled vehicle
Vadai	Savory fried snack made with grains